CHAMELEON HEART

UNVEILING THE COLORS OF LOVE, LOSS AND THE UNCHARTED PATHS OF LIFE.

ANMOL RANJAN

To all the souls who have walked this journey with me,

To those who have been my pillars of strength, offering
unwavering support,

To those who have challenged and tested me, forging my
resilience,

To those who have come and gone, leaving indelible
imprints on my heart and soul,

You have all contributed to the person I am today.

To my dear friends who have become family, and the
strangers who have shown unexpected kindness,

To the mentors who have guided me, and the critics who
have spurred my growth,

To the moments of joy and sorrow that have colored my
path,

And to all the readers who find meaning in these pages,

This book, *Chameleon Heart*, is for you.

A special thank you to my brother, Kishlay, for supporting
me through every situation. To my family—Mom and
Dad—for your unending love and belief in me. To all my
cousin brothers and sisters, thank you for believing in me
even when I was still figuring things out.

I know I might be busy and somewhat self-focused these days, but please know that I love you all dearly.

Thank you, everyone.

Contents

Foreword

The journey of life is a complex tapestry woven with moments of joy, sorrow, love, and learning. *Chameleon Heart* begins with a pivotal moment that many of us can relate to: leaving the comfort and familiarity of home to pursue secondary education. This transition marks the start of a new chapter, one that is filled with both excitement and apprehension.

Our protagonist steps into this new world with dreams and aspirations, unaware of the myriad challenges and experiences that lie ahead. The story unfolds through a series of poignant and sometimes tumultuous events that shape their path. From the thrill of first love to the pain of heartbreak, from academic pressures to the quest for self-discovery, each experience contributes to the protagonist's growth.

Please note, *Chameleon Heart* is a work of complete fiction. While it draws inspiration from real-life events and experiences—both mine and those around me—it is crafted to offer valuable life lessons and insights. The characters and scenarios are fictionalized, meant to provide guidance on decision-making and personal growth rather than reflect actual events.

Throughout *Chameleon Heart*, you will witness the protagonist's journey through the ups and downs of life. The hurdles faced, the lessons learned, and the triumphs achieved all play a crucial role in their evolution. This book is a tribute to the resilience of the human spirit and the ability to adapt and thrive in the face of adversity.

As you delve into this story, may you find reflections of your own experiences and draw inspiration from the protagonist's journey. Life is a constant ebb and flow, and *Chameleon Heart* is a reminder that with every challenge comes an opportunity for growth and with every setback, a chance for a new beginning.

I promise it will be an exciting ride.

Welcome to the journey.

Preface

"Chameleon Heart" is a tale that captures the essence of transformation and growth. Leaving home for the first time is a significant milestone in one's life, marking the beginning of an extraordinary journey filled with discovery, challenges, and triumphs. This story is a reflection of the universal experience of stepping into the unknown, navigating the turbulent waters of adolescence and young adulthood, and emerging stronger and wiser.

As you turn the pages of this book, you will walk alongside the protagonist, experiencing the highs and lows, the love and heartbreak, and the invaluable life lessons that shape us all. *"Chameleon Heart"* is not just a story; it's a mirror to our own journeys, reminding us of the resilience and adaptability inherent in each of us.

I hope this book inspires you to embrace change, cherish your experiences, and find strength in every challenge. Thank you for joining me on this heartfelt journey.

With gratitude,
Anmol Ranjan

Acknowledgements

"Chameleon Heart" has been a journey of passion, perseverance, and love. This book would not have been possible without the unwavering support of so many incredible people in my life.

To my family, your love and encouragement have been my rock. Thank you for believing in me, even when I doubted myself. Your faith in my dreams has been my guiding light.

To my friends, your enthusiasm and constructive feedback have been invaluable. Thank you for the countless hours of brainstorming sessions, late-night discussions, and the endless cups of coffee. Your support has made this journey unforgettable.

To my readers, you are the heart and soul of "Chameleon Heart." Thank you for embarking on this adventure with me. Your imagination and engagement bring these pages to life. I am deeply grateful for each and every one of you.

With all my heart,
Anmol Ranjan

CHAPTER ONE

EMBARKING THE UNCHARTED : PRELUDE TO CHANGE

As the rhythmic clatter of the train echoed through the station, I stood on the platform surrounded by a cacophony of farewells and the unmistakable hiss of departing steam. My father stood beside me, his hand resting gently on my shoulder, a knowing smile exchanged that radiated reassurance. Beside us, Vaibhav, my childhood friend with a penchant for quirky jokes and a shared love for adventure, added a touch of lightheartedness to this poignant moment.

In my hands, I clutched a pen and notebook, a conduit for the flood of memories that cascaded through my mind. The inked reflections began with the simplicity of my school life, a time when laughter echoed in hallways and friendships were unburdened by the weight of impending change. I recalled the warmth of shared jokes with Vaibhav, a reminder of the camaraderie that now faced the test of distance. Then came the pivotal decision, a familial resolve to elevate my education, leading me to the education hub of Kota.

In the midst of this emotional whirlwind, a struggle brewed within me – the excitement for new opportunities mingling with the fear of leaving everything familiar behind. The memories crystallized into specific scenes, like the echo of laughter from the schoolyard or the bittersweet tang of a goodbye hug, making the impending departure more tangible.

Fast forward to this very morning, where my mother, with a delicate touch, meticulously packed the remnants of my life into bags – a poignant and symbolic act, signaling my departure and the beginning of a journey into the unknown. As someone passionate about reading and writing, I sought solace in the familiar strokes of my pen, using it as a tool to chronicle the impending transition from the comfort of home to the uncharted territories of self-discovery.

As the train whisked me away, the solitude of the compartment mirrored the complex emotions welling within. The nostalgia of my mother's tearful goodbye resonated deeply, amplifying my solitude in this moving vessel of transition. Hesitation lingered in the air, interwoven with the threads of excitement and the overwhelming realization that my life was about to take an irreversible turn.

After an arduous journey spanning almost a day, the train finally rolled into Kota, Rajasthan, marking the initiation of a new chapter in the narrative of my life. Armed with a few addresses from well-meaning relatives, we embarked on the quest for a suitable hostel or PG. Each place fell short of our expectations, contributing to a sense of mounting uncertainty. It wasn't until the late hours that serendipity led us to a promising option – A-18 Indravihar, nestled within the confines of the Rose Royal Residency.

Despite the steep cost that loomed before us, a collective decision emerged, driven by a mix of desperation and hope. The allure of A-18 Indravihar, coupled with the pressing need for a stable accommodation, forged our path. This pivotal decision culminated in our eventual enrollment, solidifying the upcoming of my journey into the unknown.

In the twilight hours of our first day in Kota, exhaustion and hunger became our silent companions. The relentless search for a place to rest led us to a humble dinner spot, a quaint eatery with dim lighting and the comforting aroma of spices. As we replenished our energy with steaming plates of local delicacies, the ambience became the backdrop for shared stories and laughter. In that moment, we temporarily set aside the weight of our new reality, finding solace in the camaraderie forged over a simple meal.

With stomachs sated, we retreated to the unfamiliar beds in Rose Royal Residency, the lull of exhaustion attempting to lure us into a night's embrace. However, sleep proved elusive in this alien environment. The creaking sounds of a foreign dwelling and the distant hum of an unfamiliar city kept my mind teetering on the edge of slumber. Beyond the physical fatigue, the night carried an undercurrent of internal conflict, with fears and anxieties about the unknown future tugging at the edges of my consciousness.

As dawn broke, excitement spurred Vaibhav and me to explore Resonance, our academic haven. Armed with my trusty Android phone—our beacon through the labyrinth of Kota—we navigated the city's streets, our enthusiasm outpacing our weariness. Resonance loomed before us, not just as an imposing fortress but as a bustling hive of student activity. The energy, the architectural marvels, and the palpable pursuit of knowledge made it a unique realm for eager knights like us.

Fate, however, played a trick on us. The digital oracle, Google Maps, faltered, leaving us stranded in the vast unknown. Desperation etched our faces as the realization sank in – we knew the name of our destination but not the exact address. In this moment of uncertainty, a lifeline emerged in the form of a call to my father. His voice, a calming presence, guided us back on course, ensuring our triumphant return to the Rose Royal Residency.

Vaibhav, my steadfast companion, displayed a mix of emotions during the navigational mishap. While panic flickered in his eyes, his resilient spirit cracked a joke that, for a moment, lightened the weight of our predicament.

The call to my father went beyond a mere exchange of addresses. His reassuring words, beyond providing guidance, served as a reminder of the support system that bridged the gap between the familiar dreams of home and the undiscovered adventures awaiting us in Kota.

The Our second day unfolded with a mission – a seminar that promised to unravel the mysteries of our academic journey. The resonance of wisdom echoed through the hall as we absorbed the rules, including the intricate dance of batch shuffling. One particularly impactful piece of advice lingered in our minds: always carry a three-color pen, a beacon of clarity in the sea of knowledge, adding a personalized touch to our learning experience.

Post-seminar, we delved into the treasures bestowed upon us – a goodie bag bursting with essentials. creating a sensory experience that immersed us in the excitement of preparing for our academic pursuits. The jingle of the store's entrance bell, the vibrant colors' of neatly stacked supplies, and the subtle aroma of ink in the air heightened our anticipation.Energized by newfound knowledge and armed with our stationery haul, we navigated Kota's streets, treating ourselves to shakes and pani puri, absorbing the vibrant essence of this new chapter.

With the parting embrace of my father, our lives converged into a singular thread, weaving the tapestry of our independent existence in the labyrinthine city of Kota.Alone in the echoing space left by our parents' departure, Vaibhav and I found ourselves at a crossroads, contemplating the adventure that awaited us in Kota. The first order of business was to procure essentials – pens and notebooks to ink our academic journey.

As we embarked on this mission, the universe had its design. In the aisles of a nearby stationery store, we encountered kindred spirits – Siddharth and Ankit – new friends who hailed from the same building. Siddharth, with a keen eye for vibrant colors' and a penchant for organization, contrasted with Ankit's easygoing nature and love for quirky pens. Our impromptu camaraderie marked the beginning of a support system in this uncharted chapter of our lives, adding a touch of humor to the mission of buying pens that showcased each character's personality. United by the pursuit of knowledge and the common ground of Rose Royal Residency, our encounter added a comforting familiarity to this exciting yet uncertain journey.

The inaugural day of our coaching dawned upon us, and our entry into a promising batch reflected our success in the initial entrance exam. The aura of excitement and anticipation buzzed around the classrooms where remarkable teachers awaited us.

In the lecture hall, a captivating image flashed before our eyes—an enthusiastic teacher, gesticulating passionately, captured the attention of a large class of students. This visual set the tone for what awaited us – a journey infused with the charisma and passion of our educators, each weaving a tapestry of knowledge that fueled our aspirations.

On that very first day, a deluge of study materials cascaded upon us like a waterfall of challenges. A vivid image depicted textbooks and notes cascading down a table, symbolizing the overwhelming academic tasks that awaited us. Back in our room, the weight of this academic offering lingered as a reminder of the path ahead. Rather than simply stating the "weight of responsibility," I felt the tension in my shoulders and the pressure in my chest as I confronted the challenge of mastering the material.

The aroma of food wafted through the air as we indulged in our first meal, but my focus shifted to the stack of materials awaiting my attention. Determined to meet the challenge head-on, I delved into solving those study materials, each question a stepping stone toward our academic pursuit.

However, Vaibhav, ever the voice of a different perspective, disrupted my concentration. "We came here for fun, not just to study," he declared as he ventured outside. Instead of explicitly stating his words, I felt a tug at my concentration, a subtle echo of an alternate path. Yet, I remained tethered to the task at hand, the weight of responsibility anchoring me to the pages of the study materials.

The duality of purpose, one seeking knowledge and the other chasing moments of joy, unfolded in the dimly lit room of A-18 Indravihar. An accompanying image illustrated the scene – a cosy student room with books scattered, a laptop open, and soft lighting casting a warm glow.Under the shroud of night, our quest for bonding and sustenance led us to Terrence's eatery for dinner—a lively student hangout with warm lighting, food on tables, and people chatting. The sights, sounds, and smells of this place created an atmosphere of camaraderie.

In this hive of camaraderie, Siddharth and Ankit reappeared, creating an unexpected reunion. As we exchanged pleasantries, it became evident that our paths were diverging. Siddharth, a beacon of brilliance, and Ankit, a contrasting force, were enrolled in Allen, a different institute. Ankit harbored aspirations in the realm of medicine, while Siddharth aligned his ambitions with ours – engineering.

Amidst the aromatic symphony of Terrence's ambience, conversations flowed like tributaries merging into the river of shared goals. The scent of freshly brewed coffee, the gentle hum of distant chatter, and the soft strains of acoustic music wafted through the eatery, immersing us in its welcoming atmosphere.

In the midst of this sensory experience, Vaibhav's perspective on the morning walk added another layer to our shared journey. Briefly sharing his thoughts or feelings about the morning walk could provide insights into his overall approach to studies and well-being.

The next morning revealed a harsh truth – the commitment to an early start was a collective agreement but an individual endeavor. Only Siddharth and I managed to break free from the cocoon of slumber, embarking on a solitary journey through the silent streets of Kota. An accompanying image of silent, empty streets with a few dedicated students scattered about could enhance the visual depiction of our early morning walk.

The morning unveiled a tableau of determination as we encountered specific individuals scattered across parks and benches. Instead of generalizing about "young minds," a specific encounter with someone and their interaction with Siddharth or me added a personal touch to our motivation to study.

In every corner, the fervor of education became palpable, an invisible force propelling us forward into the uncharted realm of knowledge and ambition. A corresponding image of a library or students intensely studying in various locations could emphasize the "fervor of education" in Kota.

The dawn of the following day ushered in a divergence in our academic trajectories. While I prepared to face the challenges of the institute, Vaibhav opted for a reprieve, expressing his desire to take a break. Delve deeper into my own emotions regarding Vaibhav's decision, exploring whether I support it, feel concerned, or experience worry.

The web of deception tightened as the consequences of Vaibhav's absences reached beyond the classroom. The institute, vigilant in its tracking, sent a notification to his parents each time he skipped a session. Panicked calls ensued from concerned parents seeking reassurance about their son's well-being.

In the face of inquiry, Vaibhav, like a seasoned actor, played the part of an ailing student, explaining away his truancies with tales of sudden illness. A narrative of sporadic maladies became his shield against the probing questions of his worried parents.

Delving into my own emotions regarding Vaibhav's deception, I grappled with a mix of conflicting feelings. While I felt a sense of loyalty to my friend, I couldn't shake the growing unease and complicity in a deception that carried potential risks.

As the charade continued, a clandestine strategy emerged. On days when he opted for an unsanctioned hiatus, Vaibhav entrusted me, or another ally, with his student ID card. The exchange unfolded surreptitiously, with a quick, furtive pass of the card, a shared look of understanding, and perhaps a hint of tension in the air. This clandestine dance allowed him to preserve the illusion of attendance, sparing him the interrogation triggered by the institute's vigilant notifications.

The echoes of deception reverberated in the corridors of academia, a delicate dance between commitment and evasion. The potential risks weighed heavily on my mind, adding another layer to the internal conflict I experienced.

The day unfolded with formidable challenges as the institute presented intricate lessons. However, by day's end, a glimmer of encouragement emerged from our teacher – a figure with a distinctive teaching style and a knack for making complex material accessible.Amidst the intricate web of academia, our beacon of inspiration emerged in the form of Mrs. Gupta, our seasoned chemistry teacher. Mrs. Gupta possessed an air of both authority and warmth, her eyes reflecting a profound passion for unlocking the mysteries of science. With her silver-streaked hair pulled into a neat bun, she carried an air of wisdom that spoke of years dedicated to the pursuit of knowledge.

Mrs. Gupta's teaching style was akin to a skilled storyteller weaving a captivating narrative. Complex chemical equations transformed into compelling tales of atomic interactions, and periodic trends unfolded as chapters in the grand saga of the elements. Her classroom, a sanctuary of learning, echoed with the animated discussions sparked by her thought-provoking questions.

In the face of formidable challenges, Mrs. Gupta's encouragement became the linchpin that held our resolve intact. She had a unique ability to distil the most intricate concepts into digestible portions, often concluding her lessons with a nugget of wisdom that transcended the boundaries of textbooks. Her impactful words resonated in the air long after the class had ended, acting as a motivational undercurrent for our academic journey.

One memorable instance stood out when, at the end of a particularly challenging session, Mrs. Gupta shared a quote that reverberated with us all: "Understanding 30 percent of a complex concept positions you favorably on the path of knowledge. It's not about perfection; it's about progress." Her words, delivered with a reassuring smile, alleviated the weight of the academic challenges we faced, transforming the classroom into a space where growth and learning took precedence over perfection.

In the grand tapestry of our academic journey, Mrs. Gupta's role was pivotal. She not only imparted knowledge but fostered a spirit of resilience and curiosity that went beyond the confines of textbooks. Through her distinctive teaching style and impactful encouragement, she became an enduring figure in our narrative, guiding us through the labyrinth of learning with wisdom, compassion, and an unwavering commitment to our intellectual growth.As time elapsed, Vaibhav's dedication to studies dwindled, giving way to a newfound habit – smoking, a vice he now shared with Ankit. Concerned for his well-being, I attempted to steer him away from this detrimental path, but his retort stung – "You are not my guardian." The weight of disappointment and concern settled in my chest as I reluctantly withdrew, watching from a distance as he ventured into uncharted territories.

A month elapsed, bringing forth the day of batch shuffling. An examination ensued, reshaping our academic destinies. Fate had a peculiar design – I transitioned from Batch A5 to A3, a notable advancement. The elation at my progress, however, was tempered by the stark contrast of Vaibhav finding himself in Batch J5, the lowest tier. A split-screen image could poignantly depict this disparity – me proudly entering a higher batch classroom while Vaibhav looked dejected in a lower-tier classroom.

The disparity stung, and tears welled in his eyes as he vowed to improve. Despite the setback, I stood by him, offering encouragement. Delving deeper into my emotions, anger, disappointment, and concern mingled as I grappled with the unfolding narrative.In the realm of J5, a new chapter unfolded for Vaibhav, accompanied by a cohort whose ethos mirrored their own – a disdain for studies and an ardent pursuit of enjoyment. Specific incidents or interactions that exemplify the J5 cohort's priorities and lifestyle could add texture to their collective narrative.

In the depths of the lowest batch, Vaibhav's journey took an unexpected turn with the entrance of Kajal, a rebellious spirit whose penchant for defiance made her a distinctive presence. One afternoon, as the sun dipped low over the horizon, I stumbled upon an unusual sight in the courtyard of the hostel.

Kajal, with an air of nonchalance, was holding an impromptu gathering. A group of students from various batches had gravitated towards her, captivated by her bold charisma. Amidst laughter and the clinking of clandestine bottles, Vaibhav stood among them, his usual reservations seemingly cast aside.

Their camaraderie unfolded in this covert gathering, where discussions of rebellion mixed with the sweet scent of forbidden indulgence. Kajal, with a mischievous glint in her eyes, handed Vaibhav a cigarette, breaking down the barriers of his reluctance. In that moment, a subtle shift occurred – the once-dedicated student now partaking in an act that mirrored the newfound freedom he sought.

This incident, a mere snapshot in the evolving narrative, hinted at the potential influence Kajal wielded over Vaibhav. However, the constraints of her strict hostel limited the extent of her indulgences.

A curious proposition arose when Vaibhav offered his room for a clandestine rendezvous, a gateway for Kajal to experience beer for the first time. The gate's two openings conveniently masked their activities, shielding them from prying eyes and stringent regulations. As I delved into my studies, a sense of powerlessness gnawed at me, fearing the consequences of their actions and questioning my role in maintaining the delicate balance of academics.

As this covert arrangement persisted, their rendezvous evolved into a routine – a weekly escape into the realm of smoking and drinking within the confines of our room. The disapproval lingered, but my loyalty to Vaibhav restrained me from divulging this to his family. The fear of repercussions, not just on our friendship but on our academic pursuits, held me back.In a heartfelt plea, I urged Vaibhav to reconsider the frequency of these escapades, emphasizing the potential impact on our studies. Delve deeper into my anxieties and motivations regarding the clandestine rendezvous, exposing the internal conflict of fearing getting caught while feeling powerless to intervene.

Despite my concerns, the trio, Vaibhav, Kajal, and I, collectively navigated the challenges before the next batch shuffle. Despite my own mediocre transition to A6 from A3, their efforts propelled them further, transcending the limitations of the lowest batch and proving that academic redemption was within reach.

The harmony of our academic pursuits was shattered when a tempting proposition echoed through the phone receiver. Harsh, a classmate with a charismatic yet somewhat shady demeanor, painted Delhi as a haven of fun, luring Vaibhav away from Kota's relentless academic embrace. Harsh, a character with a charismatic yet somewhat shady demeanor, found himself in Delhi, short of money and there just for fun. In the labyrinth of the bustling city, where FOMO (fear of missing out) held sway, he viewed Vaibhav as the easiest bait for his own financial and entertainment needs.

Harsh possessed a cunning persuasiveness that masked his underlying motives. He recognized in Vaibhav an opportunity for financial collaboration, knowing that the allure of a different city and the promise of carefree enjoyment could cloud Vaibhav's judgment. Harsh's own financial constraints in Delhi heightened his inclination to target someone he believed could be easily swayed.

With a knack for exploiting vulnerabilities, Harsh painted an enticing picture of Delhi as a haven of fun, a place where financial concerns could be set aside for a life of excitement and revelry. His persuasive charm lay in appealing to Vaibhav's desire for a break from the relentless academic pressure in Kota and the prospect of experiencing the thrill that Delhi seemed to offer.Harsh's calculated targeting of Vaibhav showcased his opportunistic nature, capitalizing on the vulnerabilities he perceived in Vaibhav's circumstances.

Amidst the whirlwind of departure, I stood firm, my room paid for a year, shielding me from immediate consequences. The echoes of my warnings fell on deaf ears as Vaibhav ventured into a new chapter, oblivious to the potential repercussions.

Three months later, the aftermath of his decision lingered. The once-shared journey fractured, and I found myself in solitude marked by a sparse circle of study-oriented friends. Undeterred, I embraced this newfound solitude as an opportunity for undistracted focus on my academic pursuits, determined to carve a path that echoed resilience in the face of unexpected departures.In the quiet corridors of my solitary abode, the echoes of departed friends lingered. The once-shared laughter and camaraderie dissolved into the silence that enveloped my room. As I stared at the empty spaces that once held the vitality of Vaibhav's presence, the realization dawned – the ebb and flow of life's journey had taken an unforeseen turn.Yet, amidst the solitude, I found solace in the pursuit of knowledge. The hollowness of absence was filled by the weight of textbooks and the promise of academic growth. In the face of unexpected departures, the resilience of my purpose stood unwavering.The chapter closed with a resolve to navigate the challenges of Kota, not as a mere survivor, but as a scholar determined to unravel the mysteries of education. As the door to that chapter clicked shut, the unwritten pages of the next beckoned, promising a narrative that would be shaped by the choices made and the lessons learned in the corridors of Rose Royal Residency

CHAPTER TWO

WHISPERS OF DESTINY: THE UNLIKELY BOND

In the aftermath of Vaibhav's departure, a palpable void settled in our once-shared space. The silence that followed was profound, as if the very air had thickened, causing familiar furniture to feel distant, and casting unfamiliar shadows from once-familiar objects. It was within this silence that Kajal sought refuge in my room, a place where the stringent rules of her hostel couldn't deny her the freedom to indulge in her chosen vices. The specific nature of these vices remained elusive, leaving a sense of mystery.

In the quietude of my room, hesitation gripped me as I delicately expressed my concerns to Kajal. "Please don't come here," I urged, weaving a subtle plea into my words. The absence of Vaibhav lingered, enveloping the room in a shadow that reminded us both of what was once a shared sanctuary.

I emphasized the necessity for an undisturbed study environment, recognizing the subtle shift in dynamics between us. "We aren't such close friends that you should visit me," I admitted, drawing a boundary in the sands of solitude. Unbeknownst to us, destiny quietly wove intricate threads, setting the stage for an unforeseen connection that would shape our lives.

Despite my initial reluctance, Kajal's plea resonated with my compassionate side. "Just for today," I conceded, understanding her predicament of having no other place to go. She assured me that her presence wouldn't impede my studies, promising to leave early.

A week later, the echoes of her footsteps returned. On that particular day, the weight of loneliness and the relentless pressures of study burdened my mood. The fragile boundaries that I had tentatively set now faced the challenge of an unanticipated guest intruding into the sanctuary of solitude.

As the conversation unfolded, the barriers of solitude crumbled under the weight of shared stories. Amidst sips of beer and the evocative wisps of cigarette smoke, Kajal's words painted a vivid portrait of her tumultuous family background. Her father, a wealthy man owning lots of showrooms, carried the heavy burden of a daily ritual – the persistent dance with cigarettes and alcohol.

In a vulnerable moment, she peeled back the layers of her past, revealing the harsh contours of a relationship marked by a father's unyielding discipline. Her mother, a gentle soul, stood in stark contrast to the shadows cast by her father's actions. Kajal's narrative spoke of resilience, a tale of tasting the forbidden in the 8th standard, followed by clandestine forays into smoking and drinking – a rebellion cloaked in secrecy.

Amidst the smoky haze, the weight of her story settled in the room, and a connection unfurled – a shared understanding of the complexities that shape us. In her vulnerability, Kajal became more than a mere visitor; she transformed into a fellow traveler on the winding roads of life. An unexpected bond emerged in the silent spaces of my once solitary room, where the aroma of hops, the bitter fizz on the tongue, and the acrid bite of smoke heightened the sensory experience, making the connection more palpable.

In the aftermath of Kajal's revealing narrative, a moment of quiet lingered in the room as she rested before eventually bidding farewell. As the echoes of her departure faded, I found myself immersed in contemplation, thoughts weaving through the intricate threads of her story.

Yet, with the arrival of a new day and the rhythm of routine, the initial tumult settled. The mundane cadence of dinners and the quiet embrace of dawn worked their magic, restoring a semblance of normalcy. The room, once marked by solitude, became a sanctuary where the ebb and flow of study once again held sway.

However, when the following Saturday arrived, so did Kajal. A subtle shift had occurred – an unspoken anticipation for the continuation of our conversations. The routine of study was momentarily interrupted, replaced by the intrigue of shared stories and the prospect of newfound connections. The room, once a fortress of solitude, now harbored the echoes of companionship that transcended the confines of mere acquaintanceship.

In the sanctuary of our conversations, Kajal unveiled more chapters of her life's story. The narrative took an unexpected turn as she shared the heart-wrenching discovery of her father's extramarital affairs, a revelation that served as the catalyst for her journey to Kota. Despite her reluctance to study, the echoes of betrayal resonated, pushing her into the confines of an academic pursuit she never desired.

Her mother, a beacon of kindness, yearned for her presence, but the echoes of familial bonds were severed as Kota beckoned. The city became both a refuge and a battleground for Kajal, a place where academic pursuits intersected with the scars of a tumultuous past.

As the stories unfolded, she extended a gesture of camaraderie, offering me a bottle of beer. In a gentle refusal, the unspoken boundaries of personal choices were respected. Instead, we exchanged phone numbers, transcending the realm of face-to-face conversations to the virtual domain of WhatsApp. Normalcy unfolded in the pixels of our messages, occasionally punctuated by the warmth of a phone call. The connection, now spanning beyond the physical confines of my room, became a testament to the intricate tapestry of shared narratives and burgeoning companionship.

As the days unfolded, the threads of our friendship wove a tapestry of shared moments and growing intimacy. In the dance of emotions, my chameleon heart began to absorb the vibrant hues of Kajal's presence, deepening the connection between us. Her birthday became a milestone, a day etched with significance as we found ourselves as the sole companions in each other's lives.

In the effervescence of celebration, Kajal, with a spark of excitement, offered me my first sip of beer. A seemingly inconspicuous act, given the familiar backdrop of Kota's drinking culture. Yet, that singular sip became a catalyst for a night that unfolded in hues of celebration and uninhibited revelry. Additional bottles joined the scene, and the rhythmic dance of camaraderie transformed into a literal dance – an exploration of connection and shared joy.

The night unfolded, and in the haze of laughter and inebriation, Kajal chose to stay. In the embrace of the night, we ventured into uncharted territory, sharing an intimate moment that marked a first for both of us. In the aftermath of that night, a new connection emerged – a fusion of emotions and physicality that, in the tapestry of my chameleon heart, was defined as love.

In the aftermath of that transformative night, the contours of our connection underwent a profound shift. Kajal became more than a friend; she emerged as the confidante I trusted above all. The walls that once guarded my innermost thoughts crumbled, replaced by a vulnerability that found solace in the sanctity of our shared moments.

The rhythm of our days changed as she seamlessly integrated into the fabric of my life, spending more and more time by my side. What began as a friendship transcended conventional boundaries, evolving into a companionship that saw us becoming living partners. The room that once echoed with the silence of solitude now resonated with the shared laughter, whispers, and the unspoken understanding that marked the essence of our newfound connection.

With an implicit shift in our dynamics, Kajal made a symbolic move that mirrored the transformation within our relationship. She gathered her belongings, leaving behind the confines of her previous space to join me as my roommate. In the place once occupied by Vaibhav, her presence infused a new energy, a tangible testament to the changing tides of our connection.

This decision also meant a departure from the toxicity of her previous living situation. Leaving behind the tumultuous relationships with her former roommates, Kajal embraced a new chapter where the echoes of daily fights were replaced by the shared laughter and understanding that defined our evolving companionship. The room, now adorned with the traces of her presence, became a haven where the complexities of life were navigated together.

Amidst the evolving companionship, the allure of escapism began to overshadow the demands of academia. The pursuit of intoxication, a seductive dance with getting high, and the enticing tendrils of smoking became the chosen path. A divergence from the rigors of studying took root, marked by intentional absences from the institute.

In a quest for heightened experiences, the boundaries of experimentation extended to pills, seeking an elevation beyond the realms of conventional highs. The dichotomy of priorities shifted, and the pursuit of altered states became the focal point, casting shadows over the once-cherished pursuit of knowledge. As the room embraced the haze of these choices, the trajectory of our lives embarked on a precarious journey, fueled by the intoxicating allure of substances.

The consequences of our choices manifested with the arrival of the shuffling exam. Despite my sincere efforts to reconcile the diverging paths of indulgence and academic diligence, the stark reality unfolded – my grades plummeted. The stark contrast between my dwindling academic performance and the success of those who prioritized studying became an undeniable reflection of the choices we had made.

While I reveled in moments of intoxication and escapism, others dedicated themselves to the pursuit of knowledge. The divergence between the two trajectories became more pronounced, and the repercussions of prioritizing pleasure over academic responsibilities began to weigh heavily on my academic standing. The room, once a witness to shared laughter, now harbored the silent echoes of consequences, a testament to the price paid for the intoxicating detour from the path of disciplined study.

In the aftermath of the shuffling exam, a sobering realization dawned – the primary reason for our presence in Kota was slipping through the cracks. Recognizing the need for a course correction, a collective decision was made to refocus on the very purpose we had come here for – studying.

A new chapter unfolded as I took on the role of a tutor, guiding Kajal through the intricacies of the subjects from the basics. To my delight, she proved to be a quick learner, embracing the opportunity for a fresh start with enthusiasm. The room, once a witness to tumultuous nights of revelry, now echoed with the quiet cadence of shared learning, symbolizing a return to the core reason we embarked on this academic journey in the first place.

Amidst the echoes of change, our lives became encapsulated within the four walls of our shared room. A one-room existence emerged, marked by the intertwining of study sessions, moments of intoxication, and the haze of shared indulgence. The confines of our chosen sanctuary bore witness to the delicate balance of escapism and academic pursuits.

In this cocoon of shared experiences, the rituals of smoking and drinking found a place alongside the solemn pursuit of knowledge. Our existence, once defined by external distractions, now centered around the intimacy of our shared space. The outside world faded into the background as the room became a microcosm of our chosen reality – a sanctuary where the boundaries between studying, indulging, and living blurred into a seamless tapestry of one-room life.

In the crucible of shared determination, a transformation unfolded. The once daunting complex problems succumbed to the synergy of our efforts. Against the odds, Kajal ascended from the depths of the worst batch, bridging the gap to come within proximity of mine. Despite the technicalities of batch assignments, our synchronized study sessions defied the conventional boundaries, converging in the realm of shared academic pursuit.

Over the course of 8-9 months, we unraveled the intricacies of Resonance, discovering the nuances and loopholes that eluded others. Our shared understanding of the system became a formidable tool, allowing us to navigate through challenges and transcend the limitations imposed by conventional academic structures. The room, once a witness to distractions, now echoed with the resonance of triumph over academic hurdles, a testament to the transformative power of focus and shared determination.

As the months unfolded in the cocoon of our one-room life, the narrative took an unexpected turn. What began as a tale of distractions and indulgences gradually evolved into a story of resilience, shared determination, and academic triumph.

In the subdued glow of study lamps and amidst the lingering scent of smoke, we traversed the intricate landscape of knowledge. Together, we conquered the complexities that once seemed insurmountable. Kajal's journey, from the periphery of the worst batch to the proximity of mine, mirrored the transformative nature of our shared commitment to learning.

The resonance of our accomplishments echoed beyond the confines of our room, resonating with the unspoken acknowledgment of our peers. Our unconventional approach, fueled by our shared understanding of the system, became a source of inspiration for those who had once dismissed the possibility of success.

As this chapter reached its conclusion, the room, once a witness to distractions, now stood as a silent testament to the power of focus, friendship, and the unexpected turns that life takes. The next chapter awaited, promising new challenges and unforeseen twists in the journey of Kajal and me through the corridors of Rose Royal Residency.

CHAPTER THREE

Vanishing Echoes: A Heart in Shadows.

Amid the ebb and flow of our academic pursuits, a chapter unfolded marked by shared happiness and the warmth of companionship.

In celebration of our achievements and the joy that permeated our lives, we ventured to the local mall. There, amidst the bustling crowds and vibrant storefronts, Kajal, armed with the financial stability that came from her savings, unveiled a surprise that would become a pivotal moment in our shared narrative.

As we strolled through the labyrinth of shops, exploring the myriad choices the mall had to offer, Kajal's eyes gleamed with anticipation. The surprise she had in store was revealed—a sleek iPhone, a testament to her thoughtful generosity and the depth of our connection.

This unexpected gift, not just a technological marvel but a symbol of our shared triumphs, added a new layer to the tapestry of our journey. The iPhone, now an integral part of our daily lives, captured the essence of our happiness, becoming a silent observer to the joy that colored our days.

However, beneath the surface of this seemingly idyllic chapter, a subtle shift occurred. The shadows, though momentarily dispersed by the glow of happiness, began to cast a nuanced presence, hinting at the complexities that would soon unravel in the chapters to come.

In the wake of shared moments and the intoxicating highs that colored our days, a pivotal moment unfolded—a week marked by an unintended lapse. As the intoxication of the moment clouded our judgment, a realization dawned, and a subtle tremor ran through the fabric of our connection.

In the aftermath of this shared vulnerability, I recognized the potential consequences and took a step to mitigate them. With concern etched across my face, I urged Kajal to consider contraception pills—a precautionary measure intended to safeguard against the unintended repercussions of our shared intimacy.

This moment of vulnerability added a layer of complexity to our narrative. Little did we know, this pivotal point would set the stage for the vanishing echoes that would shape the trajectory of our shared existence.

In the aftermath of our shared vulnerability, Kajal responded with a sense of assurance, downplaying the urgency of the situation. "I'll take it later," she said, her words carrying a tone of familiarity based on past experiences that seemingly reassured her.

As we navigated the complexities of the moment, a subtle undercurrent of uncertainty lingered beneath the surface. The decision to defer the precautionary step became a thread in the intricate tapestry of our journey, a decision that, unbeknownst to us, would cast its shadows in the chapters that lay ahead.

In the aftermath of that pivotal moment, a sense of normalcy returned to our shared space. The bond that had weathered challenges and triumphs continued to thrive, and our academic pursuits remained steadfast. With a solid foundation of shared experiences and a deep understanding of each other's strengths and vulnerabilities, our connection seemed unshakeable.

As we delved into our studies with renewed focus, the shadows that briefly cast their presence began to recede. The intricacies of our shared journey, marked by highs and vulnerabilities, only seemed to fortify the strength of our bond. Little did we foresee that the echoes of that moment would linger, setting the stage for a narrative yet to unfold.

In the midst of our seemingly flawless days, a sudden and unexplained void emerged. Weeks of tranquility shattered when Kajal, without warning, vanished from our shared space. As the clock ticked into the late hours, I found myself waiting anxiously, my stress mounting with every passing moment.

Frantically calling her, my attempts were met with the disheartening echo of an unreachable phone. Desperation set in as I reached out to her roommates for any semblance of information. To my surprise, their response held a stark revelation—she was supposed to be living with me, not them.

A sleepless night unfolded, marked by worry and unanswered questions. For the first time, she didn't show up, leaving behind a void that hinted at the shadows looming on the horizon. The tranquility we had cultivated was replaced by an unsettling uncertainty, setting the stage for a chapter in our journey where echoes would vanish into the enigmatic abyss.

Amidst the growing worry and the echoes of her sudden disappearance, a dilemma emerged—whether to take matters into my own hands or trust in the connections she maintained with her family. The idea of involving the police crossed my mind, but the uncertainty of her family's awareness and the complexity of our young age stayed my hand.

Opting for a more patient approach, I hesitated to initiate the involvement of authorities, placing a tentative trust in the familial connections that were woven into the fabric of her daily life. Little did I anticipate that this decision would set the stage for a waiting game, a period of unanswered questions and mounting anxiety as the mystery of her disappearance lingered in the shadows.

As the week unfolded, a heavy cloud of real depression settled over me. In the absence of any trace or communication, the weight of her unexplained disappearance grew unbearable. The room we once shared, adorned with remnants of her presence—her clothes, the silent phone that refused to ring—became a haunting reminder of the void that now consumed our shared space.

Each passing day deepened the shadows of uncertainty, and the absence of answers intensified the emotional turmoil. The echoes of her sudden departure reverberated through the room, leaving me in a state of profound disquiet, grappling with the silent questions that had no apparent answers. In the midst of this emotional storm, the chapters of our shared existence were plunged into darkness, and the journey ahead seemed shrouded in an enigmatic haze.

In the isolating depths of her absence, the weight of loneliness became unbearable, and despair took hold. With her departure, she had taken with her not just a presence but the anchor of companionship. Alone in the room that once held shared laughter, I found myself ensnared by the suffocating grip of suicidal thoughts.

The profound solitude, coupled with the unanswered questions, created a haunting void that echoed with despair. In the silence of the room, the shadows of her sudden disappearance fueled a desperate yearning for answers, and the emotional toll manifested in the darkest corners of my mind. As I grappled with the overwhelming weight of despair, the shadows of the unknown loomed larger, casting a pall over the chapters of our shared journey.

In the persistent haunting of daily despair, a moment of resilience emerged. Faced with the relentless weight of suicidal thoughts, I summoned the courage to confide in my mother. Acknowledging the toll that Kota had taken on my well-being, I expressed my deep distress, revealing the shadows that had eclipsed the once vibrant echoes of my existence.

With a shared understanding and concern, a decision was made—our time in Kota, marked by the completion of the 11th standard, would come to an end. The collective agreement to bring an end to this tumultuous chapter, to abandon the haunting specter that gripped my mind, offered a glimmer of hope.

Leaving behind the shadows of despair, I embarked on a journey back home, seeking solace in the familiar embrace of family and the possibility of rebuilding a life where the echoes of my existence could resonate with a renewed sense of purpose.

Returning home marked a physical departure from the haunting confines of Kota, but the echoes of her sudden disappearance continued to reverberate through the corridors of my mind. The familiar surroundings provided a semblance of comfort, yet the uncertainty surrounding her fate cast a long and unsettling shadow.

The specter of not knowing her whereabouts or the reasons behind her disappearance persisted, leaving me entangled in a web of unanswered questions. The weight of uncertainty, coupled with the lingering emotional toll, made it challenging to find closure. Even amidst the familiar warmth of home, the ghost of her absence continued to haunt my thoughts, casting a pall over the attempts to move forward.

In the quest for solace and a fresh start, the prevailing discomfort at home led to a collective decision. Believing that the source of my unease stemmed from study pressure, my family extended support by providing funds somewhat around lakhs to enroll in a new institution, Mentors, located in Patna.

The hopeful endeavour to find a new path and redirect the trajectory of my academic journey became a collective effort, driven by the desire to lift the shadows of the past. Little did we anticipate that this decision would set the stage for a chapter where the pursuit of knowledge and healing would intertwine in unexpected ways.

In the search for closure and perhaps a glimpse into the mystery of her whereabouts, the journey to Patna unfolded. Driven by the hope of finding her in familiar territory, I ventured into the city of Samastipur. However, the vastness of the urban landscape proved to be a formidable challenge, leaving me unable to trace any signs of her presence in the bustling city.

The quest to find her became an exploration through the labyrinthine streets and corners of Patna, an endeavor marked by both determination and the ever-present shadows of uncertainty that lingered over the chapters of our shared history.

Amidst the sprawling landscapes of uncertainty and the haunting echoes of a vanished presence, the chapter drew to a close. The quest for answers had led me through the corridors of Kota, back to the embrace of home, and finally to the bustling streets of Patna. Yet, the shadows of her unexplained disappearance lingered, casting a veil over the very fabric of my existence.

In the wake of this tumultuous journey, I stood at the precipice of an uncertain future, where the threads of our shared history were woven with the enigmatic tapestry of unanswered questions. The weight of her absence and the echoes of our entwined past had become an indelible part of my story.

As the curtain fell on this chapter, the narrative remained suspended in a poignant moment of uncertainty, marking the transition from the haunting echoes of the past to the unwritten pages of the future. The search for closure and the pursuit of self-discovery would continue, casting a hopeful gaze toward the chapters yet to be unveiled in the captivating narrative of life's unpredictable odyssey.

CHAPTER FOUR

ECHOES OF NEW CITY - AND NEW CHANGES

On a bright afternoon in Patna, I embarked on a journey to the unfamiliar grounds of Mentors, the institution that would shape my academic future. The choices presented before me were a labyrinth of courses, each package promising a similar odyssey of learning. Undeterred by the potential challenges, I opted for the all-encompassing 11-12 and mains-advanced combination for the year. Cautious about the commitment, I decided to test the waters by paying for just one month, with the intention to reassess my path later.

As I contemplated an immediate return to my hometown after securing admission, the staff at Mentors had other plans. They insisted I attend the first class. With reluctance, I agreed, and as the daylight gradually gave way to evening, the class seemed to stretch endlessly. Seated next to me was Devang, a fellow aspirant whose roots were intertwined with Kajal's hometown. Feeling the pressure of time, I shared my urgency to leave.

Devang, however, saw reason in staying, given the lateness of the hour. He extended a generous offer to lodge at his PG for the night, assuring me that he would also assist in securing a more permanent accommodation the following morning. This unexpected turn of events made me reconsider my initial plan of a swift departure, marking the beginning of an unforeseen camaraderie forged in the heart of Patna.

After a prolonged night of academic introductions and camaraderie with Devang, my initial plan to return to my hometown after securing admission took an unexpected turn. Devang insisted that I stay with him in his PG for the night, assuring me that he would assist in finding a more suitable room the next morning.

As dawn broke, Devang and I embarked on the quest to find a room that would become my sanctuary during this academic journey. The options presented themselves, but the reality was less appealing than anticipated. The rooms, while budget-friendly, fell short of expectations, with their quality mirroring the less-than-ideal location.

Undeterred by the initial setbacks, Devang and I continued our search, navigating the intricate streets of Patna in pursuit of a place that would not only be a residence but a haven amidst the challenges of academic rigor. Little did I know, this exploration marked the beginning of a chapter where the city's nuances and the resilience forged through shared experiences would shape our journey in unexpected ways.

The morning unfolded with the sun casting its warm glow over the city, and as we delved deeper into the quest for a suitable abode, the true essence of Patna began to reveal itself. The vibrant street life, the eclectic mix of people, and the echoes of a city with a rich history created a backdrop for this chapter in my life.

Despite the initial hurdles, Devang's unwavering support became a beacon of comfort. Our search for a room evolved into a shared adventure, a bonding experience that transcended the mere quest for shelter. In the labyrinth of Patna's housing options, the city became not just a location for academic pursuits but a canvas upon which our journey unfolded.

As the day progressed, and our quest continued, the realization dawned that the perfect room might be elusive, but the resilience forged through the shared endeavor with Devang added a unique vibrancy to the unfolding chapter. The city, with its quirks and challenges, became the backdrop against which friendships were tested and new beginnings were woven into the fabric of my Patna experience.

In the midst of the room-hunting escapade, Devang and I found ourselves entangled in conversations that surpassed the mundane. Dreams, aspirations, and shared apprehensions about the academic year became threads in the tapestry of our budding friendship. Patna, with its complexities and charms, provided the canvas for our stories to intertwine.

As the day wore on, our search led us to different neighborhoods, each offering a glimpse into the multifaceted character of the city. The rooms may not have met the ideal standards, but the shared laughter, the camaraderie formed in the face of adversity, and the unspoken understanding between Devang and me transcended the physical aspects of our prospective abode.

By the time evening painted the sky with hues of orange and pink, we found ourselves back at Devang's PG. Despite the day's challenges, a sense of accomplishment lingered. The initial tremors of uncertainty had given way to the assurance that, with Devang by my side, Patna's unexplored terrain held the promise of growth, resilience, and unforeseen connections.

Little did I know that the city's streets, initially navigated in pursuit of shelter, would become the pathways of my personal and academic evolution. The room, while an essential part of my journey, became secondary to the friendships and shared experiences that blossomed amidst the challenges of that fateful day.

As night settled over Patna, Devang and I reflected on the day's adventures. The city, with its inherent vibrancy and the promise of uncharted opportunities, had become the backdrop for a chapter that would redefine the contours of my academic pursuit and the relationships that would shape the echoes of my time in Patna.

With the dawning of a new day, our quest for the perfect room continued. The uncertainties of the city, the shared laughter in the face of setbacks, and the unwavering support of Devang marked the early pages of a chapter that promised not just academic growth but the discovery of resilience and camaraderie in the unexplored corners of Patna.

Having navigated the intricate streets of Patna, Devang and I finally stumbled upon a room that, while not perfect, seemed like a workable abode. The trade-off was made—accepting the imperfections of the room for the promise of a shared journey and the warmth of companionship.

The room, although not situated in an ideal location, became the tangible representation of my commitment to this academic adventure. Rent was paid, marking the official beginning of my temporary residence in Patna. However, the allure of my hometown beckoned, and I made the decision to temporarily retreat and backpack my belongings.

The transition back to my hometown was laden with a mixed bag of emotions. On one hand, the room in Patna represented a newfound chapter, while on the other, my hometown held the familiar embrace of family and the comfort of the known. As I packed my belongings, I couldn't help but feel the weight of anticipation for the experiences that awaited me in Patna.

The room, though a physical space, had already become a symbolic threshold to a journey filled with uncertainties, growth, and the echoes of camaraderie. Little did I know that this decision to temporarily return home marked the closing of one chapter and the prelude to the unwritten pages that awaited me in the vibrant city of Patna.

Upon returning to Patna, the room I had secured with Devang's help became more than just a space—it evolved into a canvas awaiting personal touches and a reflection of the journey ahead. Devang, alongside his two friends sharing the same PG, generously extended their assistance in setting up my new abode.

The room, initially a blank slate, began to transform. With each item carefully placed, the echoes of camaraderie and shared experiences resonated within the walls. Devang and his friends, becoming the architects of this transformation, turned the room into a haven where the uncertainties of a new chapter in my academic pursuit began to feel a bit more like home.

As we arranged the furniture and hung memories on the walls, the room gradually ceased to be just a physical space—it became a testament to the bonds formed in the face of challenges. The shared laughter, the collaborative effort in making this space comfortable, and the unspoken understanding among newfound friends added a layer of warmth to the room's ambiance.

In the midst of arranging belongings and adjusting to the rhythms of my new life in Patna, the city itself began to feel more familiar. The room, now a reflection of shared experiences and the resilience of friendships, became a sanctuary within the bustling tapestry of the city.

Little did I realize that the setting up of this room marked more than just a practical task; it symbolized the collaborative spirit and the support system that would accompany me through the unpredictable twists and turns of my academic journey in Patna. The room, now adorned with personal touches and shared memories, stood as a tangible reminder of the unwritten chapters awaiting exploration in the vibrant city that had become my temporary home.

As the routine of academic pursuits took hold in Patna, the room that had once been a blank canvas now echoed with the quiet hum of focused study sessions. Devang and I, alongside his friends from the same PG, delved into our coursework, forming an impromptu study group within the confines of our shared academic space.

Yet, amid the pages of textbooks and the rigors of academic endeavors, the shadows of past memories cast their presence. While not entirely overwhelmed, a subtle undercurrent of nostalgia and reflection began to color the otherwise studious atmosphere of the room. The city, with its vibrant streets and the promise of new experiences, seemed to coexist with the echoes of a chapter left behind.

In the quiet moments between study sessions, as the weight of academics momentarily lifted, the room became a haven for introspection. The city lights outside the window flickered like distant stars, casting a gentle glow on the pages of open textbooks. It was in these moments that the remnants of past memories surfaced, a quiet reminder of the journey that had brought me to this point.

Navigating the complexities of study and personal reflection, the room transformed into a space where academic pursuits and the echoes of the past intersected. The city, bustling beyond the window, seemed to hold the promise of fresh beginnings, yet the layers of memories added depth to the narrative of my Patna sojourn.

As I immersed myself in the academic challenges of the present, the room became a sanctuary for both concentration and contemplation. The echoes of the past, though softened, lingered in the corners, creating a tapestry where the threads of nostalgia intertwined with the vibrant hues of the city's daily life.

In the midst of settling into the routine of academic life, there was a day when I found myself in a friend's room, contemplating a call home. As I entered my room with the intention to connect with my family, a shock coursed through me – the iPhone that Kajal had gifted me was missing, stolen in an unexpected turn of events.

The quest to recover the stolen iPhone plunged Devang, his friends, and me into a whirlwind of efforts. We meticulously searched nearby rooms, hoping for a trace of the missing device, and took the necessary step of filing a police complaint. Despite our collective endeavors, the elusive iPhone seemed to have vanished without a trace, leaving us grappling with the frustration of a situation where efforts yielded no resolution.

Faced with the disheartening loss of the iPhone, I reached out to my family, seeking solace and support. In a surprising turn of events, my father, armed with a humble keypad phone, made an appearance. The stark contrast between the stolen modern device and the simplicity of the keypad phone underscored the unexpected twists that life can present, as my family rallied around me in the face of unforeseen challenges.

In the aftermath of the phone theft, a silver lining emerged as I discovered that one of my cousin brother Shivam was residing in Patna, engrossed in his own preparations. This revelation sparked a decision – to pack my belongings from the current accommodation and move into his hostel. The shared pursuit of academic goals between us offered not only a change in living arrangements but also the promise of companionship and shared understanding during this challenging phase of our lives.

Discovering that my brother Shivam wasn't particularly strong in studies, we recognized the potential of the months left before the exams. In a strategic move, we laid out a plan to tailor our study schedules accordingly. The shared commitment to academic improvement became the driving force behind our collaborative efforts, as we embarked on a journey to support each other in overcoming the challenges that lay ahead.

As the pages of this chapter unfolded, the unexpected twists and turns became woven into the fabric of my Patna experience. From the stolen iPhone that disrupted the tranquility of my room to the discovery of my brother's presence, the journey took unforeseen routes. The decision to move into his hostel marked a shift in the narrative, with the upcoming months poised to unfold a shared chapter of academic endeavors, resilience, and the uncharted territories of brotherly camaraderie. And so, this chapter comes to a close, leaving behind the echoes of challenges faced and the anticipation of the chapters yet to be written.

41

CHAPTER FIVE

Echoes of Desolation: A Sudden Storm

In the quiet rhythms of our lives, where everything seemed to be finding its place, a sudden storm of despair emerged. Kajal's call shattered the tranquil facade, her voice laden with anguish. As she spoke, the tale of tragedy unfolded—a devastating car accident had claimed her mother's life, leaving an indelible mark of sorrow.

In the depths of her grief, Kajal received a summons from her grieving father to return home immediately. Overwhelmed by the weight of sorrow, she inadvertently shattered her phone, severing a lifeline to the world she knew. With a one-way ticket sent by her father, Kajal disappeared into the folds of anguish and embarked on a journey to a home now steeped in shadows.

Arriving home, she found solace elusive as the tendrils of grief wrapped around her. The pain of her loss compounded as she faced an environment fraught with adversity. Trapped in a cycle of torment, Kajal became a victim of domestic strife, enduring the harsh blows of life even after the crushing blow of her mother's death.

In the chapters that followed, the story wove a tapestry of heartache, depicting Kajal's struggle against the merciless tides of fate. The once-promising horizon was now marred by the shadows of tragedy and the harsh reality of her circumstances. The journey became an odyssey of survival, with each day marked by the echoes of despair and the unrelenting storm that raged within her tumultuous life.

As Kajal navigated the tempest of her shattered world, another revelation cast its shadow over her already burdened soul. In the midst of the tumult, she discovered the quiet whispers of life within her—a pregnancy that had quietly taken root over the course of 3.5 months, concealed beneath the layers of grief and turmoil.

In the initial haze of sadness and the numbing effects of her emotional journey, Kajal attributed the physical changes to the toll of sorrow, a consequence of her high emotional state and ceaseless tears. However, as the days unfolded and the harsh reality settled, the confirmation arrived—she was pregnant.

The weight of this revelation added another layer to Kajal's already intricate narrative. The life growing within her became both a testament to the resilience of existence and a poignant reminder of the cycle of life amidst the ruins of her world. The silent whispers of a new beginning emerged amidst the echoes of desolation, shaping a narrative where hope and despair danced in delicate balance.

The revelation of Kajal's pregnancy, concealed for 3.5 months amidst the tumultuous chapters of her life, echoed with profound intensity. The delicate balance between hope and despair, intertwined in this unforeseen narrative, left me in a state of bewilderment, grappling with the magnitude of emotions that unfolded within the echoes of desolation.

As the gravity of Kajal's situation unfolded, she shared her address, urging me to meet her in person. The prospect of this encounter added another layer of complexity to the already intricate tapestry of our intertwined lives, leaving me with a mix of anticipation, concern, and an eagerness to be there for her in this challenging chapter.

In haste, I made my way to Kajal's place, and upon arrival, she called me into her home. The atmosphere was heavy with an unsettling quiet, and my fear intensified when Kajal revealed that her father had been absent for days, showing little concern for their well-being. Amidst the shadows, her young sister Anjali emerged—a shy and beautiful presence in the midst of the chaos.

As the weight of the situation pressed upon us, the reality of impending parenthood, coupled with our youth and unpreparedness, led me to insist on the difficult choice of abortion. Kajal, grappling with her own emotions and the complexities of the circumstances, faced the daunting decision that lay ahead. The walls of her home held the echoes of a tumultuous chapter, where the innocence of youth clashed with the harsh realities of life.

In the midst of the overwhelming circumstances, Kajal reluctantly agreed to consider the option of abortion under one condition—that I leave my home and embark on this challenging journey with her. Despite the weight of the decision, and fueled by a shared sense of desperation and confusion, I found myself agreeing to every detail. With the resources we had—her funds and what little I possessed—we set out on a journey marked by uncertainty, a decision made in the throes of emotional turbulence and youthful naivety.

Under the weight of our decisions, we embarked on a journey away from the shadows that clung to Kajal's home. The road ahead stretched into the unknown, mirroring the uncertainty of our emotions and the challenging path we had chosen.

As we left her home behind, the backpacks on our shoulders held not only the essentials for survival but also the weight of our shared burden. The air was thick with tension, and the silence between us echoed the unspoken fears that lingered in our hearts.

In an attempt to escape the haunting memories, Kajal suggested we travel anywhere but not in Bihar, a place intertwined with painful associations. Her frustration fueled the desire for distance, and we found ourselves in Mughalsarai, now named Pandit Deen Dayal Upadhyaya Nagar—a destination that seemed like a refuge from the ghosts of our past.

In the dimly lit corners of Mughalsarai, Kajal's frustration found solace in a bottle of hardcore whisky. The amber liquid mirrored the intensity of our emotions as she drank, the burn of alcohol serving as a temporary escape from the harsh realities we faced.

Amidst the flickering shadows of our makeshift refuge, I seized the moment to reach out to my friends. Through a maze of conversations and favors, I managed to secure the contact of Manish, a friend whose connections could potentially assist us in navigating the difficult journey of abortion.

As Kajal drowned her sorrows in the numbing embrace of alcohol, I discreetly made arrangements, discussing our situation with Manish and seeking his guidance. The minutes felt like hours as we waited for a lifeline, a ray of hope in the darkness that surrounded us.

With a glimmer of possibility emerging from the shadows, I joined Kajal in the ritual of escape through intoxication. The night unfolded, shrouded in suspense, as the repercussions of our choices loomed large. The distant city lights of Mughalsarai flickered like distant stars, witnessing the unfolding drama of two young souls grappling with the consequences of a turbulent chapter in their lives.

As the whisky bottle emptied and the night deepened, we found ourselves on the precipice of a journey filled with uncertainty and complexity. The echoes of our decisions reverberated in the stillness, blending with the distant hum of the night, creating a tapestry of suspense that enveloped us in its enigmatic embrace.

In the aftermath of our desperate quest, Manish's contact led us to a doctor who, with a grave diagnosis, agreed to perform the abortion, citing Kajal's inability to give birth. The weight of the revelation hung in the air, freezing time and numbing our senses. In that moment, a profound sadness enveloped us, transcending the bounds of any pain we had felt before.

With stoic determination, Kajal, a brave soul weathering a storm, walked into the operation theater. The sterile walls held the echoes of decisions made in the crucible of despair. As I waited, every tick of the clock resonated with the heaviness of our choices.

The doctor's post-operation instructions were a stark reminder of the fragility of our existence. Kajal, now marked by the scars of both physical and emotional battles, was advised not to feel bad for a few days. The list of restrictions painted a somber picture—no shouting, no sex, and the stark permission to indulge in alcohol and smoking, perhaps as a temporary salve for wounds too deep to heal.

The burden of these instructions pressed heavily on both of us. As a young soul carrying the weight of responsibility, I nodded in agreement, yet the gravity of the situation lingered in the quiet between us.

Returning to the hotel room, the air was laden with unspoken emotions. The walls held the secrets of a tumultuous journey, and the hollowness of our shared experience echoed through the silence. In that room, shadows of the past collided with the uncertain contours of our future, creating a space where the complexities of life seemed to converge, leaving us suspended in the aftermath of choices that altered the course of our intertwined lives.

In the confined space of our hotel room, the remnants of our ordeal lingered like ghosts. The desire for a momentary escape led Kajal to the cigarettes tucked away in a corner. In her pain, she sought solace in the familiar ritual of lighting up.

With genuine concern, I gently refused her request, aware of the doctor's stern instructions. However, pain and frustration converged, turning her plea into aggression. A pot flew through the air, aimed at me as I sat on a chair. The impact stung, but understanding her turmoil, I chose not to react, absorbing the physical and emotional blows.

In an effort to bring calm to the tempest within her, I shifted gears, offering a gentle head massage. Yet, her fury persisted, a storm raging within her. Faced with the intensity of her emotions, I ultimately succumbed to her request, lighting a cigarette to ease her pain.

The room, now tainted with the scent of smoke, became a battleground for emotions too raw to be contained. In that moment, I grappled with the complexities of providing comfort in the face of adversity, navigating a delicate dance between care and self-preservation as we both sought refuge from the storm that raged within.

As the smoke dissipated, leaving behind the residue of our shared struggles, Kajal, weary from the emotional and physical turmoil, found solace in the cocoon of my arms. The weight of her pain, the echoes of our tumultuous journey, and the quiet aftermath of decisions made in desperation converged as she surrendered to sleep.

In that tender moment, I became a silent guardian, watching over her as she slipped into the refuge of dreams. The room, once a battlefield of emotions, transformed into a sanctuary where the shadows of our shared ordeal seemed to recede.

As Kajal's breathing steadied and the lines of tension softened on her face, I couldn't help but marvel at the vulnerability of the human spirit and the resilience that often emerges from the depths of despair. In the stillness of that night, the quiet cadence of her breath became a poignant reminder that even amidst the storms of life, there exists a fragile beauty—a sanctuary found in the embrace of sleep and the arms that offer solace.

As the night wore on, I remained vigilant, keeping a watchful eye on Kajal's peaceful slumber. The stillness in the room provided a strange sense of solace, a momentary respite from the chaos that defined our recent days.

However, in the midst of my silent vigil, the realization struck—I had forgotten that neither of us had eaten the night before. The morning light revealed Kajal's hunger, a reminder of the basic needs overshadowed by the complexities of our journey.

Swiftly, I ventured out to procure a nourishing meal, prioritizing protein-rich food to replenish what our bodies had lacked. The act of caring for her basic needs became a small anchor in the storm of our circumstances.

Amidst these moments, the outside world began to encroach. Anjali, Kajal's younger sister, reached out to us, her voice a lifeline from the reality we had momentarily escaped. However, the revelation that Kajal's father, upon learning of her absence, showed little concern, pierced through the fragile sanctuary we had built.

His callous words, "Let her die," echoed with a cruelty that surpassed the pain of our physical and emotional struggles. In that stark moment, the harsh reality of familial indifference became an additional burden to bear. As we faced the consequences of our actions, the outside world, with its judgments and apathy, encroached upon the fragile bubble we had crafted, forcing us to confront the harshness of a reality that seemed intent on testing the limits of our resilience.

In the quest for stability, I ventured into the realm of employment, applying for a coaching teacher position for classes 8-10. A stroke of luck, or perhaps my own resourcefulness, led me to secure the position after a brief interview. The weight of responsibility now rested on my shoulders as I stepped into the role, determined to navigate the challenges that lay ahead.

Yet, looming on the horizon was the impending storm of the 12th boards and the IIT exams, a challenge that had slipped through the cracks of our chaotic journey. The realization dawned that our educational pursuits, once promising and filled with potential, now hung in the balance.

As I juggled the demands of work and the looming academic challenges, the fragility of our situation became even more apparent. The delicate balance between securing a stable income and salvaging our educational aspirations created a tightrope that seemed perilous in the face of an uncertain future. The chapters of our intertwined lives continued to unfold, each page marked by the relentless pursuit of stability in the midst of chaos.

In the wake of a week marked by progress and the yearning for a change of scenery, Kajal expressed her frustration with being confined to the room. In response, we decided to break free from the confines, booking a cab to explore the nearby Banaras temple and Assi Ghat. The serene surroundings offered a brief respite from the weight of our shared experiences.

However, amidst the calming ambiance, a tension emerged as Kajal, seeking escape, urged me to procure alcohol. My steadfast refusal echoed both the doctor's advice and the understanding that such indulgence could jeopardize her recovery.

The clash between her desire for momentary relief and the constraints imposed by the circumstances added a layer of complexity to our journey. In the tranquil settings of Banaras, the push and pull of conflicting needs mirrored the intricate dance of hope and struggle that defined our intertwined lives. The chapters unfolded, each page etched with the delicate balance between seeking solace and navigating the constraints imposed by our tumultuous reality.

In the shadow of a fleeting victory for her desires, the night unfolded with the uncorking of the bottle. As the room filled with the scent of alcohol, the ambiance shifted, carrying with it the weight of unspoken tensions.

Amidst the clinking of glasses, Kajal's demeanor took a sharp turn. Her attempts to initiate a more intimate connection were met with my persistent refusals, grounded in the awareness of her fragile emotional state. Despite my reservations, she pressed on, becoming increasingly agitated.

The evening took a tumultuous turn as her frustration found an outlet in physical aggression and accusatory words. In the midst of her hitting and yelling, the air grew thick with the realization that the delicate balance we had tried to maintain was unraveling. The echoes of her accusation, claiming a change in me, reverberated in the confined space of our room, underscoring the strains and challenges that had woven themselves into the fabric of our shared narrative.

The aftermath of the night's storm unfolded in the harsh light of the next morning. Despite my attempts to address the chaos with calmness, Kajal, now harboring her own doubts, refused to engage in conversation. The heavy air hung with unspoken words as she declared a desire to end it all, convinced that a perceived change in me signaled a lack of love.

In the sobering light of day, the residue of our tumultuous fight cast a pall over the room. The echoes of accusations and unanswered questions seemed to linger, emphasizing the fragile nature of our relationship amidst the challenges that had tested its boundaries. The chapters of our intertwined lives took an uncertain turn, leaving us at a crossroads where the paths forward were shrouded in the haze of confusion and emotional turmoil.

The gravity of the situation reached a breaking point, and Kajal, in her anguish, made the painful decision for me to leave her home. The echoes of our shared journey seemed to unravel as I complied with her wishes, retracing the steps we had taken away from the shadows.

Leaving her home became a stark reality, a bitter pill to swallow amidst the tangled emotions that enveloped us. As the distance between us grew, the sense of loss and confusion deepened. The chapters of our story, once woven with hope and despair, now faced an uncertain future.

In the aftermath of parting ways, the weight of the situation proved too much to bear. The darkness within me led to a desperate act, and I found myself on the precipice of self-destruction. In that moment of despair, the struggle for survival became an internal battle, a solitary journey where the echoes of our shared past clashed with the harsh reality of an uncertain and tumultuous present.

In the shadows of our fractured tale, I journeyed back to Patna, seeking solace in the familiar echoes of family. The chapter closed with the weight of unspoken words and the scars of a tumultuous love, leaving behind a trail of shattered dreams and the uncertainty of what lay beyond.

CHAPTER SIX

SHATTERED HORIZONS: A SYMPHONY OF LOSS

As I returned to the familiar streets of Patna, the echoes of our shared past lingered like ghosts in the corners of my mind. The city, once a backdrop for dreams and aspirations, now held the weight of unspoken grief. Determined to find a semblance of normalcy, I embarked on a Herculean task – completing the two-year syllabus in a mere six months.

The classrooms became my refuge, the textbooks my companions in solitude. Day after day, I delved into the intricacies of subjects, the pursuit of knowledge serving as both a distraction and a balm for the wounds that refused to heal. The ambitious endeavor carried the weight of not only academic aspirations but also the burden of sorrow that lingered from the chapters left behind.

Amidst the sea of books and lectures, there was another persistent thread – the relentless effort to reach her, to bridge the distance that had grown between us. Each call became a lifeline, a fragile connection to a past where love and despair danced in delicate balance.

The juxtaposition of academic intensity and emotional longing created a narrative where the pursuit of knowledge intertwined with the echoes of lost love. As the pages turned in the book of my life, the city of Patna bore witness to a tale of resilience and renewal amidst the somber shadows of grief and the unyielding march of time.

With shared determination, my brother Shivam and I immersed ourselves in a world of books and study materials. The library became our sanctuary, the hushed tones of flipping pages and the soft murmur of whispered explanations filling the air as we delved into the academic challenges that lay ahead.

The journey of rebuilding in Patna was marked by long hours of focused study sessions. Concepts were dissected, equations unraveled, and the pursuit of knowledge became a joint endeavor fueled by a collective desire to overcome the hurdles that life had thrown our way.

Late-night discussions turned into impromptu tutoring sessions, as Shivam and I navigated the complexities of subjects together. The weight of academic expectations, once a daunting prospect, now became a shared burden, propelling us forward in our pursuit of redemption.

In the quiet corners of our home, the energy of determination mingled with the scent of midnight oil as Shivam and I forged ahead, rewriting the script of our academic journey. The shadow of past failures was replaced by the promise of a second chance, and the bond between us strengthened in the crucible of shared aspirations and relentless study sessions.

In the quiet passage of months dedicated to rigorous study, an undercurrent of melancholy threaded through my days. The academic pursuits, though promising, were tinged with the persistent ache of Kajal's absence. Each page turned and every equation solved carried the weight of a longing that refused to fade.

As the syllabus unfolded, the echo of her laughter, the warmth of her presence, and the shared dreams of a past life lingered in the corners of my consciousness. The pursuit of knowledge became a dual journey – one aimed at conquering academic challenges, and the other, an ongoing quest to bridge the emotional chasm that had widened between us.

Depression, like a silent companion, cast a subtle shadow over the triumphs of each milestone achieved. The vibrancy of the study sessions contrasted with the muted colors of a heart that missed her presence. In the solitude of late-night study sessions, the emptiness echoed louder than the whispered explanations of textbooks.

Yet, amidst the turmoil of emotions, the commitment to academic resurrection remained steadfast. The pursuit of knowledge, now coupled with the persistent hope of reconnection, shaped the narrative of these months—painting a canvas where the triumphs and struggles blended into a poignant portrait of resilience.

With the shadows of academic uncertainty hanging over us, the certainty of passing 12th was a glimmer of hope. However, the elusive goal of cracking the IIT exam cast a veil of doubt on our aspirations. Amidst these academic concerns, my worry for Kajal loomed large.

The streets near her home witnessed my presence twice, a silent pilgrimage of concern. Despite the yearning to check on her well-being, the weight of rejection in her unreturned calls held me at the threshold. The courage to step inside, to face the echoes of a love now entangled with silence, eluded me.

The chapters of our lives unfolded in tandem—academia and the unresolved emotions for Kajal, each page marked by the uncertainty of what lay beyond. The backdrop of exams and unspoken emotions painted a narrative where the pursuit of success intertwined with the lingering questions of a love story left hanging in the balance.

In the crisp cold of January, as the finals loomed closer, an unexpected interlude presented itself. My brother, Shivam, exuding newfound confidence in his academic endeavors, proposed a temporary escape from the world of textbooks and numerical problems. Amidst the pages of physics equations, he suggested a respite—a visit to a nearby garden for a spontaneous photoshoot.

Initially hesitant to break the rhythm of study sessions, I resisted the idea. However, persistent insistence from Shivam, coupled with the allure of a momentary diversion, eventually swayed my decision. The cold air outside beckoned, promising a brief reprieve from the intensity of exam preparations.

Thus, in the midst of academic pursuits, we found ourselves stepping into the refreshing embrace of the garden. The click of the camera, the crunch of frozen grass beneath our feet, and the play of winter sunlight on the leaves became a temporary departure from the structured routine of study sessions.

In that spontaneous interlude, amidst the physics problems and the winter chill, the garden photoshoot etched a memory—a brief pause in the relentless march towards academic goals, a snapshot capturing a moment of camaraderie amid the pages of textbooks and the quiet resolve to face the upcoming challenges.

In the wake of our impromptu garden photoshoot, an unexpected turn of events cast a shadow over the fleeting joy. That very night, Shivam's laughter was replaced by the grimace of stomach pain. Concern etched across his face, he grappled with the sudden onset of discomfort.

In an attempt to alleviate his suffering, I suggested the simplicity of lukewarm water, hoping it would offer some relief. Little did we know that this night, marked by a brotherly bond and shared moments of respite, would soon become a pivotal chapter overshadowed by the stark realities of health and the fragility of our transient happiness.

The night that began with laughter in the garden took a sinister turn, shattering the fragile joy. Around 3 AM, I was jolted awake by Shivam's agonizing cries, the stomach pain escalating beyond his control. A sense of urgency seized the air as I swiftly carried him to the nearest government hospital.

The eerie stillness of the night was punctuated by the indifferent murmurs of doctors engaged in casual chit-chat, oblivious to the escalating gravity of the situation. Urgency coursed through my veins as I pleaded for immediate attention, the ticking clock amplifying the tension that hung in the sterile air.

In the hurried shuffle, Shivam was ushered into a room for examination. The minutes stretched into agonizing hours as I sat outside, my anxious heart pounding in sync with the ominous ticking of the clock on the wall. Questions went unanswered, and a disconcerting silence enveloped the hospital corridors.

As the night wore on, the weight of uncertainty pressed heavily on my shoulders. In desperation, I reached out to an elder brother living nearby, hoping for guidance and intervention. His arrival at around 7 AM marked a desperate plea for clarity in the disarray that had unfolded.

Frustration boiled over as my elder brother confronted the doctors, demanding the attention and urgency that seemed conspicuously absent. The veneer of calm shattered, revealing the intense worry that had been gnawing at my core.

It was then, in the stark light of dawn, that the doctors reluctantly divulged the severity of Shivam's condition. A critical diagnosis hung in the air, thick with despair. The words "transfer to Delhi" echoed with a sense of urgency, but time, a merciless adversary, refused to yield. The gravity of the situation unfolded in a tragic crescendo, leaving me entangled in a web of emotions—anguish, frustration, and an overwhelming sense of helplessness.

In that hospital room, the air became stifling, charged with the foreboding reality that our world was unraveling. The battle against time had commenced, and as the sun rose over the horizon, casting its indifferent rays on our plight, the narrative shifted into a bleak symphony of tragedy and despair.

In the midst of the nocturnal chaos, a frantic call to Shivam's parents brought them rushing, fury etched across their faces. Determined to seek more specialized care, we transported him to a private hospital, a beacon of hope in the bleak landscape of despair.

The hospital corridors echoed with urgency as we hurriedly maneuvered through the maze. The doctor's prescription hinted at the gravity of the situation, recommending a stretcher for the ascent to the second floor. However, Shivam, clinging to the vestiges of strength, brushed off the suggestion, insisting on taking the stairs.

In the urgency of the moment, we ascended to the emergency ward. The clinical precision of the surroundings seemed at odds with the tempest that raged within our hearts. Within the hour, a disquieting revelation unfolded—Shivam's kidney had ceased its function, a harbinger of a cascade effect that would soon claim other vital organs.

The harsh reality morphed into a tragic tableau as the medical team, in a desperate bid to salvage what remained, initiated dialysis. The rhythmic hum of the machinery resonated with the silent plea for a miracle. Yet, as the minutes ticked away, a devastating sequence of diagnoses followed – his liver, once a resilient organ, had surrendered to the onslaught, and the cruel hand of fate had stilled the workings of his brain.

In the hushed corridors of the hospital, the gravity of the situation became palpable. A hushed whisper echoed through the sterile air—Shivam was now connected to a lifeline, a machine mirroring the vital functions of his failing organs. The once-bustling emergency ward transformed into a surreal battleground, where medical professionals fought valiantly against the ruthless grip of multiple organ failure.

The term "brain death" resonated like a mournful refrain, casting a chilling pall over our desperate hope. Dialysis, akin to a mechanical heartbeat, sustained his failing body, painting a stark contrast to the fragility of life that now hung by the thinnest of threads.

In the relentless ebb and flow of medical efforts, we clung to the cold, unforgiving benches of the hospital, a silent chorus of grief enveloping our weary hearts. For 48 excruciating hours, the sterile hospital walls witnessed the symphony of medical interventions and our silent vigil. A cruel fate had cast its shadow, and in the poignant silence that followed, Shivam slipped away.

The announcement echoed with a hollow finality, leaving behind the resonant emptiness of a life extinguished too soon. The cold hospital room, once a battleground of desperate hopes, now stood as a poignant witness to our collective sorrow. As the reality of his passing settled like a heavy fog, the weight of sadness pressed upon our chests, leaving us entangled in the tapestry of grief that had woven itself into the fabric of our lives.

In the hallowed halls of the hospital, the echoes of whispered condolences and the quiet rustling of medical charts became a somber background to the harsh reality of loss. The chapter closed not with the triumph of resilience but with the bitter taste of grief, marking the end of a story that had started with laughter in a garden and concluded with the silent symphony of mourning hearts.

These days were the darkest chapters of my life. In losing Kajal and my brother Shivam, I felt as though the very fabric of my existence had unraveled. Broken and shattered, I stood at the crossroads of grief and despair, haunted by the memories of a love story left incomplete and a bond severed too soon.

With exams looming just a month away, the prospect of academic pursuits felt inconsequential in the face of this dual loss. Nights blurred into days as I fought against the merciless grip of sleeplessness, and life, once vibrant and full of promise, now felt like an endless descent into hell.

The weight of sorrow pressed upon me, an unrelenting force that seemed to suffocate any remnants of hope. As I navigated the labyrinth of grief, the echoes of laughter in a garden and the warmth of brotherly camaraderie seemed like distant echoes from a life that existed in a parallel universe.

In this desolate chapter, where the pain of heartbreak and the sting of loss mingled, I grappled with the profound emptiness left in their absence. The days stretched into a seemingly infinite expanse of darkness, and the prospect of moving forward felt like an insurmountable task.

As the chapter drew to a close, the narrative hung in the silence of my shattered world. These were the worst days of my life, a period where the threads of joy and love had frayed, leaving behind a tapestry woven with the threads of grief and a haunting awareness of the fragility of life.

CHAPTER SEVEN

SHATTERED DREAMS :UNVEILED

In the bleak aftermath of losing my brother Shivam and the mysterious disappearance of Kajal, my life lay in disarray, marked by the harsh reality of grief and financial destitution. The impending exams, once a beacon of hope, now loomed as a daunting challenge amidst the wreckage of shattered dreams.

As the exam season approached, I found myself standing at a crossroads. The weight of sorrow bore down on me, overshadowing any semblance of motivation to continue studying. In the last two months leading up to the exams, I made a poignant decision to halt my studies, as the relentless echoes of loss and despair reverberated through each day.

Despite my fractured state, the exam center for my 12th-grade exams remained in my hometown—a cruel twist of fate that compelled me to confront the ghosts of my past as I entered the examination hall. The first day brought with it the Mathematics paper, and as I stared at the unfamiliar questions, an unexpected flood of memories engulfed me.

Images of my friend and the now-vanished Kajal surfaced in my mind, their faces intertwined with the mathematical problems before me. I couldn't escape the vivid recollections of collaborative problem-solving sessions and shared laughter that once echoed through the halls of academia.

Frustration gripped me as the weight of their absence intensified. In a moment of despair, I made a radical decision – I left the entire paper blank. The echoes of forgotten dreams, intertwined with the haunting images of lost companions, were etched into the silent pages of my incomplete exam booklet.

The act of leaving the paper blank, born out of frustration and a profound sense of loss, became a silent rebellion against a world that had crumbled around me. In that moment, the pursuit of academic success took a backseat to the tumultuous journey of grieving and rebuilding, creating a narrative where the boundaries between despair and defiance blurred into a poignant tableau of resilience in the face of overwhelming odds.

In the subsequent days, the procession of exams continued, each paper a stark reminder of the fractured reality that had become my life. Physics and Chemistry, once subjects of fascination and exploration, now served as mere vessels for the echoes of sorrow that reverberated within.

The exam halls transformed into silent arenas where the clash between academic expectations and the tumultuous emotions within me played out. As I gazed upon the blank pages, the questions seemed like distant echoes, their significance drowned in the sea of grief that engulfed my every thought.

Whether I penned a single word or allowed the pages to remain pristine, I couldn't say. The once-vibrant journey of learning and intellectual curiosity had been replaced by a silent struggle, where the weight of heartache eclipsed the importance of academic pursuits.

In the hushed corridors of the exam center, the tension was not just confined to the ticking clock and the rustling of exam papers. It was a battleground where the intangible battles of mourning, despair, and the relentless pursuit of moving forward converged.

As the final exams drew to a close, I emerged from the halls with an air of emptiness—an indelible sense that the pursuit of knowledge, once a source of solace and inspiration, had become a casualty in the collateral damage of personal tragedy. The future seemed uncertain, and the results of these exams, while looming on the horizon, felt like distant echoes in the vast expanse of a life profoundly altered.

The passing days unfolded in a haunting silence, a realm where words seemed to dissipate before they could find utterance. The heavy weight of grief hung in the air, casting a pall over the once-vibrant home that now echoed with the hollowness of loss. Even my parents, with concern etched across their faces, believed my silence was a byproduct of witnessing the sudden demise of my roommate, Shivam.

The specter of death had woven itself into the fabric of my daily existence, leaving me ensnared in a labyrinth of thoughts and emotions. Conversations felt like a distant echo, their resonance drowned in the profound stillness that enveloped my world. The once-familiar walls of home became silent witnesses to the inward turmoil, where words failed to bridge the chasm of grief that separated me from the world.

While my parents sought to provide comfort and understanding, the language of sorrow is often one that transcends spoken words. It became a solitary journey, navigating the corridors of mourning, where even the simplest interactions felt like an insurmountable task. Each day blurred into the next, marked not by conversations but by the quiet symphony of solitude.

In the deafening silence, the unspoken grief became a palpable presence, shaping the contours of my existence. The reasons for my reticence, hidden beneath layers of sorrow, remained veiled from those who longed to understand. The mere act of speaking felt like an intrusion into the sacred space of mourning, where the language of the heart communicated in the silent echoes of shared memories and unshed tears.

Amidst the somber backdrop of grief and silence, a pivotal moment approached—the IIT mains exam, a beacon of passion and aspiration that had weathered the storm of personal tragedy. Despite the heavy shroud of sorrow enveloping my days, the embers of fervor for this prestigious examination still glowed within.

As the date loomed closer, I found myself caught in the intricate dance between the yearning for academic achievement and the weight of a heart laden with loss. The IIT mains, once a symbol of intellectual triumph and potential, now became a testament to resilience, a silent vow to pursue dreams even in the wake of shattered realities.

The examination hall, usually a battleground of intellect and determination, now bore witness to the silent struggle within. The questions, like enigmatic riddles, beckoned me to unravel them amidst the turbulent sea of emotions. The passion that had fueled my preparations clashed with the specter of grief, creating a poignant juxtaposition within the confines of that sterile room.

Each pen stroke on the answer sheet carried not only the weight of academic proficiency but also the echoes of a journey fraught with personal tribulations. The IIT mains, a crucible of intellect and ambition, became a canvas where the brushstrokes of sorrow and determination blended into a complex tapestry of the human experience.

In the midst of loss and the pursuit of passion, the IIT mains exam became a poignant chapter—a juncture where the indomitable spirit within me endeavored to rise from the ashes of despair. The resilience to face the challenge and chase the dream, despite the profound sadness that clung to my every step, spoke volumes about the human capacity to endure and seek solace in the pursuit of knowledge and personal growth.

The fateful day of reckoning arrived, bearing the weight of anticipation and anxiety—the day when the results of my endeavors would be laid bare. As I navigated through the labyrinth of emotions, the outcome became an inevitable reflection of the tumultuous journey that had defined this chapter of my life.

The results, when they finally materialized, painted a stark reality—one that echoed with the harshness of failure. In the 12th-grade board exams, I stood on the precipice of academic disappointment, scoring a mere 1 mark in Mathematics, 2 in Chemistry, and 3 in Physics. The cumulative weight of these scores felt like an indictment, each mark a testament to the challenges that had eclipsed my academic pursuits.

The IIT mains results, with their cold numerical precision, cast a further shadow on my aspirations. Instead of the triumph I had envisioned, the score of -35 reflected not only a failure to meet the academic benchmarks but also a descent into negative territory—a metaphorical plunge into the abyss of disappointment.

The weight of these results pressed upon me, a tangible manifestation of setbacks and personal tribulations. As the gravity of failure settled, the journey through the halls of academia, once paved with aspirations, now became a winding road of shattered dreams and unfulfilled potential.

In the aftermath of this academic storm, the silence that had permeated my days deepened. The specter of disappointment, woven into the fabric of my results, became a haunting companion in the midst of a landscape marked by broken dreams and the relentless echoes of loss.

In the wake of academic disappointment and the lingering shadows of personal tragedy, the decision to retreat from the world for an entire year emerged as a contemplative response. The weight of shattered dreams and the burden of grief had become too cumbersome to carry amidst the expectations of the external world.

The prospect of a self-imposed exile became a sanctuary—a space where the cacophony of judgments, expectations, and the relentless march of time could be momentarily silenced. The intention was not to halt life but to carve a breathing space within the chaos, allowing the wounds to heal and the soul to find solace in the cocoon of solitude.

As I retreated into this self-imposed exile, the days unfolded like a quiet symphony, marked by introspection, healing, and the gentle pursuit of self-discovery. In the cocoon of seclusion, the process of untangling the threads of grief from the tapestry of my identity began—a necessary step in the journey toward reclaiming a sense of self and purpose.

The world outside continued its relentless pace, but within the boundaries of this voluntary isolation, time moved at a different rhythm—a rhythm attuned to the needs of a heart in convalescence. The year unfolded not as a pause in life but as a deliberate choice to recalibrate, rejuvenate, and re-emerge with a newfound resilience forged in the crucible of personal trials.

In this self-imposed hiatus from the world, the silent dialogue with myself became a therapeutic endeavor, an exploration of the contours of my own strength and the dormant possibilities waiting to be unearthed. The decision to step away was not an act of surrender but a strategic retreat, a conscious choice to realign and gather the fragments of a shattered existence.

As the seasons cycled through their familiar dance, the cocoon of solitude served as a chrysalis, sheltering the metamorphosis within—a transformative journey where the echoes of failure and loss were gradually supplanted by the whispers of self-renewal and the promise of a yet-unwritten future.

And thus, within the cocoon of solitude, a chapter of introspection and healing unfolded. Life, akin to a novel with its unpredictable twists, had led me to this juncture—an intersection of loss, disappointment, and the resilience to seek solace within.

In the silence of this self-imposed exile, the narrative of my journey underwent a subtle metamorphosis. The meaning of this chapter lay not in the mere passage of time but in the deliberate pause to mend the fragments of a fractured soul.

As the year wove its quiet tapestry, the cocoon held the promise of transformation, echoing the resilience that emerges from embracing the complexities of human existence. With each passing day, the echoes of failure and loss faded, making way for the gentle whispers of self-renewal and the anticipation of a new chapter yet to be penned. The cocoon, once a refuge, now stood as a testament to the beauty that can emerge when one finds the courage to pause, reflect, and emerge anew.

CHAPTER EIGHT

Silent Odyssey: A Journey Within

Being out of the scope of everyone, I closed myself in a room—a self-imposed exile from the cacophony of the world. The walls became both my fortress and my confidante as I embarked on a journey of solitude, a silent odyssey within the chambers of my own existence. The weight of sorrow, the haunting echoes of failure, and the shadows of my past formed the backdrop of this lonely sanctuary.

In the dim light of isolation, I confronted the formidable adversaries of depression and despair. The room, once a mundane space, transformed into an arena where I waged battles against the demons that lurked in the recesses of my mind. The silence, profound and heavy, was both an ally and a tormentor—an ally in offering solitude, a tormentor in amplifying the whispers of my own thoughts.

The study materials became my companions, and the pages of textbooks turned as though narrating tales of resilience and intellectual conquests. The pen, now an instrument of catharsis, traced intricate patterns on the canvas of blank notebooks, translating the chaos within into a structured pursuit of knowledge.

Phones, the conduits to a world outside my self-imposed exile, lay untouched. Even in the face of complex problems, I refrained from reaching for the solace they offered. The digital world, with its myriad distractions and reminders of a life I sought to forget, remained at bay. In this intentional deprivation, I sought refuge, a means to cleanse my mind of the noise and clutter that had clouded my existence.

The isolation, though suffused with an air of melancholy, became a canvas for self-discovery and healing. The hours merged into days as I delved into the depths of subjects, challenging my intellect and, in turn, battling the shadows that sought to pull me into the abyss of desolation.

The solitude became my cocoon, a crucible of transformation where the echoes of failure gradually yielded to the whispers of resilience. The room, once a mere enclosure, became a sanctuary where I grappled with the complexities of my past, laying the groundwork for a future yet to unfold. In this silent odyssey—a journey within—I sought not only academic redemption but a profound rebirth of the self, a narrative where the chapters of despair would eventually give way to the promises of a new dawn.

While I immersed myself in the solemn seclusion of my silent odyssey, an uncharted territory of grief and self-discovery, Kajal existed in a parallel universe, blissfully unaware of the tumult that marked my world. The tendrils of my brother Shivam's death and the echoes of academic failure had not reached her, and in return, I remained oblivious to the unfolding chapters of her life.

In the cocoon of her own existence, Kajal navigated the currents of time and circumstance, a lone voyager on a separate journey. The news of Shivam's demise and the weight of my academic struggles were veiled from her, and the intricacies of my personal turmoil remained concealed beneath the surface of our disconnected realities.

As I grappled with my demons within the confines of my solitary room, Kajal danced to the rhythms of an unfamiliar melody, one untouched by the somber notes of loss or the dissonance of academic setbacks. Her world, though separate, bore its own complexities, its own set of shadows that remained hidden from my view.

The unspoken pact of distance and silence, unintentionally maintained by both of us, formed an invisible barrier between our lives. The fragments of my existence were not woven into the tapestry of her narrative, and vice versa. The intricacies of our respective struggles unfolded in isolation, each of us grappling with the weight of our own burdens, oblivious to the silent echoes of the other's journey.

This narrative of parallel lives, unbeknownst to each other, introduced a poignant dimension to our intertwined story. The universe, with its cosmic indifference, allowed our paths to diverge, weaving a tale where the threads of our lives remained separate yet intricately connected in the tapestry of shared memories.

The symphony of our individual struggles played on, and in the corridors of our solitude, we continued our journeys—each note, each step, and each revelation waiting to harmonize in the chapters that lay beyond the current veil of ignorance. The pages of our shared narrative turned quietly, yet the anticipation of eventual convergence lingered—a promise that the strands of our stories, though unraveling in solitude, might one day intertwine in a narrative of shared understanding and shared healing.

In the tapestry of our separate lives, unknown to me, Kajal embarked on her own quest to bridge the chasm of silence that had inadvertently grown between us. Unaware of the depths of my struggles, she sought to trace the footsteps of a connection severed by the twists of fate.

In her pursuit, Kajal reached out to the threads of our shared past, contacting Vaibhav, a figure from the canvas of my childhood. Vaibhav, once a bridge between my present and my roots, held fragments of my story that remained concealed from her. However, the currents of communication had waned, and the link that once bound us together had faded into the recesses of time.

Kajal's attempts to trace me, to unearth the whereabouts of a soul navigating the labyrinth of solitude, were met with the echoes of my failure. The news of my academic setbacks had severed even the last tethers of connection that Vaibhav held, leaving her with unanswered questions and a quest shrouded in uncertainty.

The echoes of her efforts, unheard in the corridors of my silent exile, added another layer of complexity to the unfolding narrative. While I immersed myself in the shadows of my own struggles, Kajal, unbeknownst to me, ventured into the realms of the past, attempting to decipher the puzzle of my disappearance.

The cosmic dance of missed connections and untold stories continued, as Kajal's endeavors mirrored my own silent odyssey in their solitary pursuit. Little did we both know that the threads of our lives, though seemingly disparate, were woven into the grand tapestry of shared history, awaiting the moment when our narratives would once again converge.

In the intricate web of our interconnected lives, the dynamics took an unexpected turn as Vaibhav, once a friend who had witnessed the blossoming of our connection, found himself grappling with unforeseen emotions. The shifting sands of our relationships left behind a trail of complexity, with Vaibhav caught in the undertow of unresolved feelings and uncharted territories.

As Kajal reached out to him in her earnest quest, Vaibhav, perhaps swayed by the currents of nostalgia and lingering sentiments, found himself in a delicate position. The lines between friendship, past connections, and newfound emotions blurred, casting shadows over the intentions that guided his actions.

Unaware of the intricacies of Kajal's journey, Vaibhav, in his attempt to navigate the terrain of emotions, found himself entangled in a dilemma. The past, once clear and defined, now became a tapestry woven with threads of complexity, as the specter of my presence and the shared history cast a shadow over their interactions.

The unfolding drama, a subplot in the overarching narrative, added layers of tension and ambiguity to the story. As Kajal sought solace and connection, she unknowingly entered a realm of emotional intricacies, where the past intertwined with the present, and friendships harbored unspoken complexities.

The cosmic dance of emotions, tangled and unresolved, continued its silent performance, unbeknownst to all parties involved. Little did Vaibhav realize the depth of Kajal's journey, and little did Kajal fathom the uncharted territories that lay ahead in the maze of rekindled connections and evolving emotions. As the threads of our interconnected lives continued to weave their complex patterns, the unfolding drama hinted at a future where the shadows of the past might cast ripples on the waters of the present.

In the backdrop of Kajal's unwavering resolve and Vaibhav's unexpected demands, a tense and unsettling drama unfolded, painting shadows on the canvas of their interactions. Kajal, standing firm in her principles and resisting any compromise of her values, found herself entangled in a web of emotional manipulation.

As Kajal sought connection and information in her quest to trace my steps, Vaibhav's intentions took a disconcerting turn. The innocent pursuit of friendship became clouded by the insidious demand for a compromise that went against the very core of Kajal's convictions. In the shadows of such unwarranted expectations, Kajal found herself at a crossroads where her principles clashed with the murky waters of Vaibhav's intentions.

The unfolding drama, unbeknownst to me in the solitude of my silent odyssey, cast Kajal as the unsuspecting protagonist in a narrative marred by emotional manipulation. The pressure to succumb to compromising circumstances, solely for the sake of gaining access to my contact information, bore the hallmarks of a disconcerting twist in her quest.

Misguided by Vaibhav's actions, Kajal grappled with the belief that this was somehow part of a plan orchestrated by me—an unwitting puppet master pulling the strings from the shadows. Little did she know that the complexities of this subplot were beyond my comprehension, a dramatic turn playing out in the background of my silent retreat from the world.

As the curtains lifted on this unfolding drama, the emotional tension thickened, leaving Kajal to navigate a treacherous terrain where the quest for connection became entangled in the snares of manipulation and emotional demands. In the complex dance of emotions and hidden agendas, Kajal's resilience faced its sternest test, all while I remained oblivious to the storm brewing in the backdrop of our intertwined stories.

The passage of time, marked by a year of separation, revealed divergent trajectories in our journeys. As I immersed myself in the solitude of self-discovery and recovery, the complexities of Kajal's quest and Vaibhav's misguided intentions continued to unfold in parallel, unbeknownst to me.

In this silent interlude, I found solace in study and introspection, gradually mending the fractures left by the trials of the past. The cocoon of solitude had become a crucible for my renewal, and as I emerged from its confines, the echoes of failure began to fade, replaced by the whispers of resilience.

Meanwhile, Kajal faced the tumultuous currents of her own challenges. The shadows of Vaibhav's ill-intentioned demands cast a pall over her academic pursuits, intertwining the quest for connection with the weight of manipulation. The relentless pursuit to trace my steps had inadvertently led her into a labyrinth of emotional turmoil, where resilience and vulnerability clashed in a silent struggle.

Vaibhav, entangled in his own web of misguided intentions, saw his academic aspirations crumble alongside Kajal's. The consequences of his actions reverberated not only in his academic standing but also in the trust he had eroded through the ill-conceived demands placed upon Kajal.

As we all stood at the intersection of failure, the divergence in our responses became apparent. The year of separation became a crucible for individual growth—a testament to the transformative power of solitude. While I reclaimed fragments of my identity, Kajal grappled with the aftermath of a pursuit tainted by manipulation, and Vaibhav faced the repercussions of intentions gone awry.

The culmination of a year marked by individual growth and triumph unfolded as the specter of academic evaluations revisited our lives. In the corridors of examination halls, I confronted the ghosts of past failures armed with newfound resilience. The silent odyssey within the cocoon of solitude had proven transformative, culminating in success as I not only secured good grades in the 12th board but also triumphed in the IIT examination.

However, the narrative took a contrasting turn for Kajal and Vaibhav. The shadows of their previous failures cast a lingering pall over their academic pursuits, as the echoes of the past reverberated in their results. The dance of fate, intricate and unpredictable, seemed to hold them captive in the relentless cycle of setbacks.

As the pages of our stories turned, the dichotomy in our trajectories became apparent. The year of separation had shaped each of us differently, molding our responses to the challenges presented. My triumphs were juxtaposed against their continued struggles, creating a tableau of success and failure within the intricate tapestry of our interconnected lives.

The convergence of our narratives remained elusive, obscured by the veils of circumstance and individual choices. The cosmic dance of fate, ever enigmatic, continued to weave its threads, leaving the eventual intersection of our stories an open-ended question in the chapters yet to unfold.

In the aftermath of triumph and success, as I reached for the familiar glow of my phone, the digital realm became a conduit to reconnect with the fragments of my past. Around one year of messages, unanswered calls, and untold stories lay dormant, waiting to be unraveled.

As I sought to bridge the gap that time and silence had forged, I discovered a narrative tainted by half-truths and unspoken complexities. Vaibhav's revelations hinted at Kajal's attempts to reach me, but the shadows cast by his ill-intentioned actions remained veiled in silence.

Upon reaching out to Kajal, the attempt to mend the threads of our connection was met with an unexpected barrier. The specter of Vaibhav's actions had sown seeds of mistrust, and the fear of manipulation echoed in her reluctance to engage in dialogue. Misunderstandings, fueled by the unspoken truths that lingered in the background, stood as insurmountable barriers to communication.

In the poignant silence that followed, Kajal, shrouded in her own perceptions, chose to distance herself from the echoes of our shared past. The desire to shield herself from potential harm became a poignant refrain, leaving our attempts at reconciliation suspended in the limbo of miscommunication.

With the weight of unspoken words and the echoes of misunderstanding, the chapter closed on a note of unresolved tension. The intricacies of our entangled lives remained suspended, waiting for the moment when the cosmic dance of fate would weave a path towards understanding and closure.

CHAPTER NINE

FRESH BEGINNINGS: COLLEGE UNCHARTED

We left Patna Airport and landed in the vibrant city of Jaipur, also known as the Pink City, where my journey at IIT Sitapura would unfold. The morning sun bathed the campus in a warm glow as I stepped into the realm of possibilities. The echoes of success in clearing the IIT exam resonated within me, a key unlocking the doors to a promising future.

The journey to this moment was a family affair – my brother, father, and mother joined me in Jaipur. Together, we explored the vibrant streets, the intricate architecture, and the soulful flavors of the city. From the mesmerizing Hawa Mahal to the regal Amer Fort, every corner of Jaipur whispered tales of history and culture.

Our journey through Jaipur became a tapestry of experiences, from the tantalizing aroma of street food to the intricate designs of traditional handicrafts. The Pink City left an indelible mark on us, a prelude to the adventures awaiting in the academic corridors of IIT Sitapura.

After a day filled with exploration, we settled into a hotel, the anticipation of the next day tingling in the air. The following morning marked my first step into the world of IIT Sitapura. The excitement was palpable as my family and I navigated the bustling streets, absorbing the unique charm of Jaipur.

Orientation day at the college brought forth a myriad of faces, each a chapter waiting to be written in the book of my college life. The syllabus, like a treasure map, hinted at the challenges and adventures that awaited.

Among the myriad of introductions, a chance encounter with Ritvik and Ishan sparked the beginning of unique camaraderies. With a shared passion for coding and a curiosity to explore the uncharted realms of computer science, Ritvik, Ishan, and I embarked on a journey through the intricacies of algorithms and the magic of programming languages.

Little did I know, as we navigated the corridors of our college, this single day held more than just academic pursuits. It was a tale of discoveries, shared ambitions, and the forging of bonds that would stand the test of time.

After that eventful day, I returned to the hotel room, the echoes of Jaipur's charm lingering in my mind. The following day unfolded as another chapter in the Pink City's story. I explored the architectural marvel of Jal Mahal, a palace seemingly floating on the tranquil waters. The historical Nahargarh Fort stood proudly on the Aravalli Hills, offering panoramic views of the city below.

As my parents bid farewell and returned home, I ventured back to the college grounds. The anticipation of starting my journey at the hostel added a new layer of excitement. The hostel, a mosaic of dreams and ambitions, welcomed me into its fold.

In the Hostel room, I met my two roommates – Sohail and Sunny. Sohail, with aspirations in electrical engineering, hailed from Kota, a city known for its coaching centers and academic fervor. Sunny, on the other hand, brought the essence of Sikar, a town rich in history and culture, with a background in civil engineering.

Our first introduction set the stage for a diverse and dynamic camaraderie. Sohail's anecdotes from Kota echoed the competitive spirit, while Sunny's tales of Sikar added a cultural tapestry to our conversations. In that shared space, we became not just roommates but allies in navigating the uncharted territories of college life.

The hostel became a hub of shared experiences and late-night discussions, where dreams mingled with laughter, and ambitions intertwined with the clatter of keyboards. Together, we faced the challenges of the academic landscape, each day writing a new chapter in our collective story.

As the days unfolded, the hostel became more than just a residence; it transformed into a sanctuary of friendships, laughter, and the shared pursuit of knowledge. The corridors echoed with the diversity of voices, each adding a unique melody to the symphony of college life.

Little did I know, as I settled into the rhythm of hostel life, that the bonds formed in those early days would become the foundation of enduring friendships. And so, the journey through the first year continued, a narrative waiting to unfold with every turn of the page.

As I entered the lecture hall on the first day of college classes, a familiar sight greeted me – Ritvik and Ishan, the friends I had made during the joining day. Without hesitation, I gravitated toward them, finding a row of seats where we could embark on this academic adventure together.

The professor's introduction echoed through the hall, but in that sea of faces, the presence of friends provided a reassuring anchor. As the class delved into the subject matter, Ritvik, Ishan, and I shared knowing glances, exchanged subtle nods of agreement, and occasionally suppressed shared laughter at a witty comment.

The synergy of sitting with friends transformed the lecture hall into a space of shared learning and camaraderie. Discussions flowed effortlessly, and the exchange of ideas felt like an extension of the connections formed during the events leading up to the first day of classes.

As the professor navigated through the syllabus, our trio became a microcosm of the larger classroom, where friendships seamlessly blended with the pursuit of knowledge. Interactive discussions gained an extra layer of familiarity, and the collective curiosity of our small group mirrored the broader enthusiasm of the entire class.

When the bell marked the end of the first class, Ritvik, Ishan, and I stepped out into the corridor, energized by the intellectual exchange and eager for the courses that lay ahead. The bond forged during that class was more than a shared seat – it was a foundation for the academic journey we would navigate together.

In the hustle and bustle of the college corridors, we shared reflections on the class, exchanged thoughts on the upcoming assignments, and reveled in the collective experience of stepping into the realm of higher education.

In the days that followed, as the college routine settled into a familiar cadence, my attention veered toward a quiet presence in the midst of the bustling class – Avani. In a sea of faces, she stood out not for her words but for her silence.

I couldn't help but notice that Avani, a girl with a voice as soft as a whisper, was consistently marked absent due to her low-tone "present, sir" during attendance. It intrigued me how someone so reserved could easily slip through the routine checks of attendance.

As the days progressed, my heart nudged me to break the silence that surrounded Avani. One day, as the professor called out names for attendance, I seized the moment. With a clarity that resonated through the room, I said, "Avani is present, sir."

In that instant, a quiet gratitude flickered in Avni's eyes, a subtle acknowledgment of being seen and heard. The small act, like a gentle ripple, created a connection that transcended the confines of the attendance register.

As the weeks unfolded, Avani and I exchanged occasional smiles, transforming the silent nods into a silent camaraderie. Our interactions were subtle, yet they spoke volumes about the power of recognizing someone in the midst of the crowd.

Little did I know, in those few moments, a friendship had begun to blossom, founded on the simple act of marking attendance. Avani's silent presence became a reminder that sometimes, the quietest voices carry the most profound stories.

In the midst of the college routine, the unspoken connection with Avani lingered, a silent thread weaving through the chapters of my new academic journey. Yet, the weight of an unresolved past cast its shadow, prompting Ishan, Ritvik, and me to seek solace and camaraderie beyond the classroom.

One evening, as the sun dipped below the horizon, we found ourselves atop Nahargarh Fort, a historical fortress that stood sentinel over Jaipur. The cool breeze and the panoramic view became the backdrop to a moment of relaxation and shared stories.

Chilled beers in hand, we exchanged tales of our hometowns, dreams, and the struggles that brought us to this juncture. The fort, with its centuries-old stones, became witness to the unburdening of our minds, a cathartic release from the weight of our pasts.

Yet, as the laughter echoed through the ancient walls, I found myself holding back, still hesitant to unravel the intricacies of my own story. Kajal's silent presence, too, remained an unspoken chapter, a mystery that lingered in the corners of my mind.

The fort, with its timeless ambiance, became a sanctuary where the complexities of life momentarily faded away. Ishan, Ritvik, and I forged memories, painting the night with laughter and shared aspirations. In the midst of newfound friendships, the past, though not forgotten, loosened its grip, allowing room for the present to breathe.

As we descended from Nahargarh Fort, the city lights glittering below, I realized that some stories need time to unfold, and perhaps, in the chapters yet to come, the unspoken tales would find their voice. The fort, our temporary refuge, stood witness to a night of camaraderie, a respite from the echoes of the past, and a gentle reminder that, in time, the unspoken could become shared chapters of trust and understanding.

As months unfolded, the routine of classes became a familiar rhythm, yet the unspoken connection with Avani persisted. In a quiet moment during a Computer Aided

Machine Drawing (CAMD) class, our paths intersected.

As the professor delved into the intricacies of drawings and designs, Avani turned to me, a soft request escaping her lips for an eraser. In that instant, I fumbled through my bag and handed it to her with a genuine smile, a silent exchange that spoke more than words ever could.

Despite the simplicity of the eraser exchange, the significance lingered. It became a subtle bridge, an unassuming gesture that hinted at a shared understanding. Yet, the dilemma of the past still clung, a silent barrier preventing the words that longed to be spoken.

In the quiet confines of the CAMD class, surrounded by the hum of machines and the rustle of papers, I wrestled with my own hesitations. The eraser, a symbol of shared moments, held the promise of a conversation yet to unfold.

As the class continued, the unspoken lingered like a melody beneath the surface. Avani and I, bound by the threads of mutual acknowledgment, continued our silent dance in the ebb and flow of the academic routine.

Little did I know, that eraser exchange would become a metaphor for the untold stories waiting to be shared, and the chapters of understanding that, in time, would find their way into the narrative of our connection. The CAMD class, with its intricate drawings and subtle exchanges, marked another layer in the tapestry of unspoken camaraderie, hinting at a future where words might finally bridge the gaps of our pasts.

As the evening settled, the glow of the day's experiences lingered in the air. To my surprise, a new message illuminated my WhatsApp screen, a Hello greeting with my name cleverly scrambled in each word. It was Avani, reaching out in a way that blended familiarity with intrigue.

Her message carried a question, a subtle request for a shared memory. Did I remember what the professor said to us as we left the class last time? The memory, vivid until that moment, momentarily slipped from my grasp until her message brought it back into focus.

With a sense of pleasure and a touch of amazement, I replied, recounting the professor's words. In that exchange, a new chapter unfolded – not just of shared academic moments but of a connection that ventured beyond the bounds of routine.

As Avani and I continued our conversation, the barriers of the unspoken seemed to dissipate, and the dialogue expanded beyond the confines of the classroom. Each message became a brushstroke, painting a canvas of understanding and shared experiences.

In that moment, the echoes of the past and the present converged. Avani's text, like a gentle breeze, carried the promise of conversations yet to unfold, bridging the gap between the unspoken and the spoken with the simple exchange of words. The evening, once marked by erasers and drawings, now held the promise of a connection that went beyond the classroom, a connection woven with the threads of shared memories and the anticipation of stories yet to be told.

As the rhythm of college life unfolded, a buzz of excitement filled the air with the approaching Engineers Day. The stage was set for students to showcase their innovative projects, and among them, Mayra, Yash, and I were fueled by a collective enthusiasm.

In the corridors of creativity, we embarked on the journey of crafting a project that would leave an impression. Together, we meticulously developed a working model of a smart shoe – a fusion of technology and practicality. The shoe incorporated sensors for health monitoring, a smart navigation system, and even an embedded fitness tracker.

The days leading up to the event were a whirlwind of collaboration, late-night brainstorming sessions, and the clatter of tools shaping our vision into reality. My expertise in programming, Yash's knack for engineering, and Mayra's contributions in design harmonized seamlessly.

On the day of the Engineers Day event, the exhibition hall echoed with the hum of creativity. Our smart shoe, standing proudly amidst an array of projects, drew curious glances. As we explained its features and demonstrated its capabilities, a sense of pride enveloped our team.

The culmination of our efforts reached its pinnacle when the announcement echoed through the hall – our project had clinched the first prize. The elation that swept through us was not just about the recognition; it was a celebration of teamwork, ingenuity, and the joy of turning an idea into a tangible success.

Mayra, Yash, and I stood together on the stage, the glow of victory mirrored in our smiles. The Engineers Day became more than an event; it became a chapter in our collective journey, a testament to the potential that thrived within the collaboration of creative minds.

In the aftermath of the celebration, we reveled in the recognition, each step in our smart shoe project symbolizing not just progress in technology but also the bonds forged through shared aspirations. The victory, etched in the annals of our college memories, propelled us forward into a future where innovation and collaboration were the guiding stars of our journey.

In the quiet aftermath of our triumph at Engineers Day, a subtle change unfolded beneath the surface.

Unbeknownst to me, Mayra's admiration for our shared success evolved into something more. It was in the midst of our joyous celebration that she mustered the courage to express what had quietly taken root.

One day, as we lingered in the glow of our achievement, Mayra approached with a warmth that hinted at unspoken sentiments. With a gentle smile, she asked if I would join her for a date. The proposal, wrapped in the sweet victory of our project, carried a sincerity that couldn't be ignored.

Caught off guard by the unexpected turn of events, I found myself grappling with the realization that a bond beyond friendship had bloomed. The recognition of Mayra's feelings brought with it a mix of emotions – surprise, curiosity, and a subtle flutter of anticipation.

Amidst the backdrop of our shared success, the prospect of a date became a chapter waiting to be written. It was a moment where the lines between achievement and personal connection blurred, and the narrative of our college days took an unforeseen turn.

As the echoes of our triumph resonated, Mayra's invitation lingered in the air, a quiet melody weaving through the tapestry of our shared journey. The date, an uncharted adventure, beckoned as the next chapter in a story that unfolded not just in the corridors of academia but also in the delicate nuances of human connection.

In the quiet aftermath of our closeness, Mayra unraveled the tapestry of her past, revealing secrets that echoed the haunting tale of Kajal. The weight of these revelations pressed upon me, casting a shadow that nearly consumed my thoughts. For a fleeting moment, I found myself slipping into the depths of despair.

Attempting to escape the turmoil, I reached out to Kajal once more, only to be met with the frustration that clung to her like a relentless storm. Recognizing the need for solace, I decided to withdraw, granting her the space to find peace within herself.

As the echoes of our connection faded into silence, I grappled with the lingering emotions, searching for a path forward. The journey ahead seemed uncertain, and the threads of our stories entwined in a delicate dance, leaving me yearning for resolution in the chapters yet to unfold.

In the labyrinth of our deepening friendship, an ominous cloud cast its shadow as a sinister misunderstanding unfolded. Mayra's digital realm became the battleground, invaded by an unseen foe who hijacked her account, manipulating it to their whims. Personal pictures became pawns, and email recovery paths were twisted, entangling my existence in this web of deception.

Suspicions arose like a tempest, and Mayra, in a quest for truth, delved into the intimate spaces of my phone. A frantic search ensued, each moment amplifying the strain on our connection. As her scrutiny revealed no trace of complicity on my part, the revelation cast a chilling light on the puppet master orchestrating this intricate play.

Our friendship, now tested by forces beyond our control, stood at the precipice of uncertainty, leaving us to navigate the aftermath of this digital tempest and rebuild the trust that had been shaken to its core.

In the aftermath of the unfounded suspicions, Mayra, burdened by unseen wounds, distanced herself. A somber day arrived when she sought my phone, a request loaded with the weight of unspoken farewells. In a decisive act, she erased the echoes of our shared moments, each deleted chat a silent requiem for what once was.

The weight of her departure hung heavily, and as the specter of misunderstanding lingered, I chose silence over confrontation. Broken by the earlier tumult, I let her go, allowing the echoes of our connection to dissipate into the void. In the quiet aftermath, the remnants of our unspoken words lingered, and the tale of our fractured friendship unfolded like a bittersweet melody fading into the recesses of memory.

In the stillness that followed, the chapters of our intertwined stories drew to a reluctant close. Unseen forces and misunderstandings had etched wounds upon our friendship, and the weight of unspoken words hung in the air.

Mayra, having chosen to sever the fragile threads that bound us, left behind a void tinged with both sorrow and acceptance. In the hushed aftermath, I faced the silent echoes of our shared experiences, allowing the narrative to conclude with a poignant sense of closure.

As the chapters folded into the past, the lessons learned and scars borne became the ink that penned the tale of a friendship tested by the unpredictable whims of fate. And so, with a heavy heart, I turned the page, knowing that the next chapter awaited, yet uncertain of what lay ahead.

CHAPTER TEN

HARMONY IN WHISPERS: WHERE HAPPINESS UNFOLDED

In the quiet echoes of my brokenness, a fragile stability anchored itself in the form of Avani. Though not the conventional definition of beauty, she possessed an ethereal allure that transcended physicality. Her charm lay in the subtle curves of her smile, the way her eyes held an ocean of emotions, and the grace with which she moved through life.

Avani's beauty wasn't a loud proclamation but a quiet symphony, playing softly in the background of my existence. Each glance revealed the poetry of her existence, and every fleeting moment with her unfolded like a delicate dance of light and shadow.

She wasn't adorned with the flamboyance that draws instant attention, yet there was an undeniable magnetism in the simplicity of her being. Avani, with her unassuming elegance, became the canvas upon which my heart painted a portrait of admiration and affection. In her presence, the winds whispered tales of enchantment, and I found solace in the gentle cadence of her existence.

Indeed, in the tapestry of imperfections, Avani emerged as a masterpiece of perfection. Her essence, a blend of flaws and virtues, created a mosaic that resonated with an unparalleled beauty. To me, she was not just perfectly imperfect; she was perfectly perfect in her uniqueness, a symphony that harmonized with the rhythm of my heart.

In the sacred space of our conversation, I chose the role of a silent listener, allowing Avani's words to weave a tapestry of comfort around my wounded soul. As the delicate dance of conversation unfolded, I couldn't resist sharing the shadowed corridors of my recent past with Mayra.

Avani's response was a gentle breeze, a soothing melody that echoed wisdom. "Remain calm and look ahead," she advised, her words carrying the weight of experience. "She'll decide if she wants to return, and if not, she loses a gem—yet not you." Each syllable she uttered felt like elixir, a remedy to the ache within, as if her words held the power to mend the fractures of my heart.

In the intricate tapestry of their digital connection, Avani, captivated by the melodies spun by her online companion, found herself drawn deeper into a relationship that transcended the boundaries of screens. The musician's tales of financial despair, claiming days without food, became a poignant plea that echoed through the pixels of their conversations.

Driven by a compassionate heart, Avani, using her own pocket money, became a lifeline for this distant troubadour. Each transaction carried with it the weight of her empathy, as she sought to alleviate the hunger he professed to endure. The strings of her generosity resonated in the digital symphony they composed together.

However, beneath the surface of this seemingly altruistic exchange, a dissonance emerged. The once harmonious notes of their virtual connection began to fray as the musician's frustration manifested in angry outbursts. Avani, caught in the delicate interplay of empathy and discord, navigated the complexities of a relationship that existed solely in the intangible realm of the internet. The allure of a virtual connection and the palpable strains of reality collided, leaving Avani to grapple with the blurred lines of compassion and the unsettling reality that unfolded within their digital dialogue.

As the realization dawned upon me that Avani was ensnared in a web of emotional and financial exploitation, I treaded carefully through the delicate terrain of her trust. Recognizing her perception of this connection as a manifestation of love, I approached the situation with the utmost sensitivity, aware that a misstep could sever the fragile bonds we shared.

Avani, a sanctuary of trust in my college life, held a unique place in my heart. In her, I found not just a friend but a confidante, someone with whom I could share the depths of my thoughts. From the very first day, she had been an embodiment of perfection in my eyes, a sentiment I had never experienced before.

Fearful of jeopardizing our friendship, I embarked on the challenging task of gently unraveling the truth to Avani. Armed with subtle proofs, I delicately exposed the manipulative threads that wove through their digital interactions. It was a delicate dance of words, an attempt to free Avani from the clutches of a relationship that concealed ulterior motives beneath the veneer of love.

In the unfolding drama of unraveling truth, the deceptive orchestrator behind Avani's virtual connection discovered my discreet efforts to guide her towards clarity. A direct confrontation ensued, a barrage of abusive language hurled through the digital waves.

In the face of his verbal onslaught, I chose silence, a stoic stance in defense of the respect I held for Avani. Each insult flung my way became a testament to the unraveling truth, reinforcing the urgency of liberating her from this toxic entanglement. The digital battlefield became a realm where words clashed, and I stood as a silent guardian, steadfast in my commitment to shield Avani from the storm of negativity that raged in the wake of our revelations.

Faced with the sinister turn of events, the manipulative figure behind the screen escalated his tactics, resorting to the despicable act of blackmailing Avani with compromising pictures. The unfolding nightmare forced me to take a reluctant step back from Avani's life, a painful retreat to shield her from further harm.

In the shadows of this digital warfare, my withdrawal became a strategic maneuver, an attempt to protect Avani from the collateral damage of this emotional turmoil. The threads of our connection strained under the weight of the circumstances, and I grappled with the helplessness that accompanies watching a friend navigate a dark labyrinth of manipulation and deceit. The decision to step back, though agonizing, was driven by a desperate hope that it might offer Avani the space she needed to extricate herself from the clutches of this emotional extortion.

In the aftermath of a tumultuous confrontation with the manipulative figure, Avani sought refuge in the midst of tears and vulnerability. The gravity of the situation had become palpable, and she reached out, expressing a heartfelt desire for my help in liberating herself from the toxic entanglement.

Amidst the echoes of her emotional turmoil, a flicker of hope ignited. In that moment, our connection, though strained, found renewed purpose. Together, we forged a pact to disentangle Avani from the clutches of the manipulator who had cast shadows upon her digital world. The battle wasn't just hers; it became a shared endeavor, a testament to the strength of a friendship weathered by trials.

As we embarked on the journey to reclaim Avani's peace, our bond, though tested, proved resilient. The fight against manipulation became a joint crusade, a testament to the enduring power of friendship in the face of adversity.

In the delicate dance of fate, Avani's heartfelt proposition unfolded against the backdrop of a momentous revelation. As the weight of manipulation lifted, the winds, as if choreographed by destiny, began to weave a gentle symphony, carrying whispers of newfound beginnings.

Avani, in the vulnerability of that moment, not only proposed a shared journey but also unveiled the depth of her emotions with tears glistening in her eyes. The winds, now more than mere elements of nature, seemed to carry the essence of our shared dreams.

In the tapestry of our connection, I, too, surrendered to the emotional current, recounting the intricacies of my past relationships and the hurdles that had defined my journey. Avani, amidst the soft rustle of the winds, embraced each revelation with a grace that mirrored the gentleness of the breeze. It was a poignant exchange, where vulnerability became the bridge connecting our pasts, leading us toward a shared future.

As she proposed, tears became the silent witnesses to the sincerity of her emotions, and in that vulnerable moment, I found myself saying yes, not just to her proposal, but to the promise of a new chapter written in the ink of understanding and acceptance. The winds, now carrying a serenade of joy, bore witness to the birth of what would become the best moment of our intertwined lives.

In the embrace of a newfound relationship with Avani, the world transformed into a canvas of endless possibilities. The weight of past trials seemed to dissipate, and a sense of invincibility washed over me. It was as if a long-cherished dream had materialized into reality, and the euphoria of conquering not just personal hurdles but the entire world became an exhilarating reality.

Avani, with her unwavering acceptance and the promise of shared tomorrows, became the beacon that illuminated the path ahead. The journey, once fraught with challenges, now seemed like an adventure waiting to be explored hand in hand. In the warmth of our connection, I discovered a newfound strength that echoed the sentiment of having the world at our feet—a testament to the transformative power of love and shared dreams.

In the enchanting realm of our blossoming relationship, the college corridors became a canvas where the tapestry of camaraderie and shared aspirations unfolded. Avani and I, united by a newfound connection, embarked on a journey that extended beyond the realms of romance, delving into the corridors of academia.

In the hallowed halls of learning, we ventured hand in hand through the complexities of classes, immersing ourselves in the challenges of programming and the intricacies of mathematics. Each lecture became an opportunity for shared exploration, as we exchanged insights, navigated through the nuances of algorithms, and collaborated on unraveling the mysteries of mathematical equations.

Post-classes, our academic synergy continued to blossom. In the heart of the college campus, we sought the comfort of round tables where the echoes of our discussions lingered in the air. These round tables, witness to the unfolding chapters of our academic endeavors, became a symbol of shared learning and the joy derived from overcoming intellectual challenges together.

The routine of studying side by side was punctuated by laughter, the satisfaction of conquering programming puzzles, and the shared sense of accomplishment when grasping the intricacies of mathematical concepts. It was a journey where love and learning intertwined seamlessly, and the college campus became not just a backdrop but an integral part of our shared narrative.

In the vibrant tapestry of our college life, the hostel became the backdrop for countless adventures, each chapter etched with the thrill of shared escapades. One unforgettable night, as residents of the hostel, Sohail, Sunny, and I decided to venture beyond the confines of our campus and embrace the allure of the unknown.

Underneath the moonlit sky, we embarked on a daring escapade, navigating the winding roads with a sense of exhilaration. Our chosen steed was a scooty, carrying us through the silent night, the hum of its engine harmonizing with the whispers of the wind. Our destination: Bhangarh Fort, renowned as one of the most haunted places in India.

As we reached the eerie surroundings of the fort, the air thick with a sense of mystery, our adventure took an unexpected turn. A vigilant guard intercepted our journey, momentarily halting our expedition. Undeterred, fueled by youthful daring, we decided to circumvent the obstacle. Climbing hills, navigating the shadows, we forged ahead, determined to create memories that transcended the ordinary.

The night unfolded as a symphony of laughter, shared secrets, and the palpable thrill of exploring the unknown. The ghostly reputation of Bhangarh Fort became a backdrop to our shared adventure, each step echoing with the camaraderie of kindred spirits on an unforgettable journey. The echoes of that night lingered, not just as a daring escapade but as a testament to the indomitable spirit that bound us together.

In the vibrant tapestry of our inaugural year at college, each chapter unfolded with a resonance that transcended the boundaries of academics. Our shared abode in the hostel, a microcosm of camaraderie and shared experiences, emerged as the backdrop for tales that added an extra layer of excitement to the canvas of our college journey.

Nights in the hostel weren't merely transitions into sleep; they were the setting for spontaneous escapades that wove themselves into the fabric of our memories. Amidst the hum of daily life, laughter echoed through dimly lit corridors, and late-night conversations became the lifeblood of our budding friendships. The hostel, with its single room light serving as the spotlight, witnessed impromptu midnight feasts and the forging of bonds that went beyond the confines of academic pursuits.

One extraordinary day stands out as a beacon in our hostel adventures. Fueled by spontaneity and a collective daring spirit, we decided to explore the nearby hills, a serene location that offered breathtaking views and an escape from the hustle of college life. The camaraderie of hostel mates, the shared laughter, and the serenity of the hilltop created memories that would forever be etched in the chapters of our shared collegiate journey.

As the sun dipped below the horizon, casting hues of orange and pink across the sky, we realized that these shared adventures were the threads that wove the narrative of our first year together. With eager anticipation, we stepped into the unwritten pages, ready to embrace the excitement that each new adventure promised in the continuing saga of our collegiate tale. The hostel, with its shared laughter and camaraderie, became not just a place of residence but a cherished setting for the stories that defined our college journey, offering a glimpse into the countless chapters waiting to unfold.

CHAPTER ELEVEN

BLOSSOMING BONDS: SOPHOMORE SYMPHONY

The arrival of the 2nd year at college marked a significant juncture in our lives, triggering a series of changes that would redefine the contours of our shared journey. As the academic landscape shifted, so did the settings of our daily lives. For me, the decision to bid farewell to the familiar college hostel and opt for a residence outside heralded a chapter of newfound independence and uncharted experiences.

Settling into my new abode, the walls resonated with the echoes of change, and the air seemed charged with the anticipation of the unknown. The room, though devoid of the comforting faces from the previous year, held the potential for new connections and unforeseen adventures. It became a canvas awaiting the brushstrokes of experience to paint the evolving narrative.

In a parallel yet contrasting decision, Avani chose to maintain her residence within the college hostel. The decision marked a divergence in our daily environments, but it also added a layer of complexity to our evolving relationship. The space between us became not just physical but symbolic, creating a dynamic interplay of closeness and distance that would shape the unfolding chapters of our shared story.

As the cityscape embraced us with its bustling streets and dynamic energy, the dichotomy of our living arrangements became a backdrop against which the saga of our 2nd year commenced. Little did we know that these changes in our living situations would set the stage for a journey of deepening relationships, unexplored emotions, and the intertwining of our individual paths within the vibrant tapestry of college life.

The city of Jaipur became our playground, and with each passing day, Avani and I delved deeper into its vibrant tapestry. Beyond the silver screens, our evenings were painted with laughter and shared joy as we strolled through the lush parks and vibrant markets, making every moment count.

Wandering hand in hand through iconic landmarks like World Trade Park (WTP) and Jawahar Circle, we unearthed the hidden gems nestled within the city's labyrinth. The vibrant hues of Jaipur seemed to reflect the kaleidoscope of emotions that colored our journey—each street corner holding the promise of a new adventure, every monument echoing the laughter that filled the air.

Our explorations weren't just about traversing the physical landscape; they became a journey into the realms of our hearts. In the heart of Jaipur's chaos, we discovered pockets of serenity, shared secrets beneath the starlit skies, and found solace in each other's company. The city, once unfamiliar, now felt like an extension of our shared dreams.

For me, every day was a dream come true. Avani's presence was the magic wand that transformed routine into extraordinary. The laughter that echoed in the vibrant bazaars, the shared glances in the shadow of historical monuments, and the quiet moments in the parks—each facet of our explorations wove a narrative that mirrored the depth of our connection.

As we explored the city together, Jaipur became more than just a location on the map; it became a backdrop to our love story. Every step was a testament to the dream that unfolded before my eyes, with Avani by my side—a realization that dreams, when shared, become a reality more enchanting than one could ever imagine.

In the ensuing year, the academic landscape underwent a transformative shift, infused with a newfound sense of joy and camaraderie. With Avani by my side, the once-daunting realm of studies became a shared adventure, every textbook page turned with laughter echoing in the background. The classrooms, once solitary, now resonated with the symphony of our shared pursuit of knowledge.

Every corner of the college seemed to radiate the energy of our collaborative efforts. Whether it was deciphering complex algorithms in programming classes or unraveling the mysteries of calculus in the hallowed halls of mathematics, our partnership transcended the boundaries of academia. The library, once a silent witness to individual struggles, became the arena where our shared intellect and mutual support flourished.

Together, we navigated the challenges of academia, seamlessly complementing each other's strengths and bolstering one another in moments of doubt. Our studies became not just a solitary endeavor but a joint venture, a testament to the strength of our connection.

As the academic year progressed, it became increasingly evident that our partnership extended far beyond the confines of textbooks and lecture halls. The support, understanding, and shared goals created a cocoon of companionship, rendering the need for external validation or interference obsolete. It was as if the universe conspired to bring us together, making it feel like we didn't need anyone else in our lives but each other—an unspoken understanding that our shared journey, both in academics and in love, was a tapestry woven with threads of mutual support and unwavering companionship.

Even amidst the harmonious symphony of our shared journey, the occasional discordant notes of disagreement crept in. Yet, what set our relationship apart was the remarkable speed with which any discord was transformed into harmony. Avani's extraordinary maturity and intelligence became the soothing balm that swiftly healed any fractures that appeared in the fabric of our connection.

In those moments of disagreement, she wielded the twin weapons of wisdom and understanding, navigating through the complexities with an effortless finesse. The conflicts, like passing storms, left no lasting impact as the skies cleared, revealing the unshakeable foundation of our relationship.

Her ability to swiftly comprehend, empathize, and communicate transcended the norm, transforming our disagreements into opportunities for growth and deeper understanding. It was a testament to the strength of her character and the resilience of our connection—each conflict only serving to reinforce the unspoken understanding that, together, we could weather any storm and emerge stronger on the other side.

In the ebb and flow of our relationship, these moments of discord became not stumbling blocks but stepping stones, shaping our journey in a way that accentuated the beauty of our connection. In the canvas of our shared narrative, the occasional brushstroke of disagreement only added depth and richness, making our love story all the more profound.

In the sanctuary of our connection, I discovered a profound transformation within myself. While I had been a closed book to the world, in Avani's presence, the barriers around my heart crumbled. With her, I found a refuge where vulnerability was not a weakness but a shared strength, and authenticity became the language of our intimacy.

In her gaze, I felt seen in ways that went beyond the surface, as if she held the key to unlocking the chapters of my soul. The walls that shielded my deepest thoughts and emotions seemed to dissolve, and I became an open book in the library of our shared experiences.

Our connection fostered an environment of trust, where I felt not just heard but truly understood. With Avani, I found the courage to unveil the nuances of my inner world, sharing dreams, fears, and aspirations. The vulnerability that unfolded became the thread weaving through the tapestry of our love story, forging a connection that transcended the superficial.

In the alchemy of our relationship, I realized that being an open book wasn't a surrender of privacy but an embrace of authenticity. Avani's presence created a safe space where every page of my story could be laid bare, and in return, I discovered the beauty of reciprocating that openness, creating a narrative that was both shared and profoundly personal.

In the tender embrace of our relationship, Avani became not just a confidante but a pillar of support as I grappled with the shadows of my past. Struggling with a penchant for cigarettes and alcohol, I found in her an unwavering ally, ready to walk with me through the journey of overcoming these challenges.

Breaking free from the clutches of addiction is no easy feat, but with Avani's steadfast encouragement, the process became more manageable. Her support was a gentle but firm guiding force, offering a light in the moments when the path seemed shrouded in darkness. The addiction, once a formidable adversary, began to lose its grip, making room for a healthier, more balanced lifestyle.

Though the journey was not without its bumps, and occasionally the familiar habits resurfaced, the remarkable transformation lay in the moderation and the newfound ability to navigate stress without succumbing to these vices. Avani's support wasn't just about breaking free from the chains of addiction; it was about creating a space where I could address the root causes, finding healthier coping mechanisms, and fostering a sense of resilience.

With her by my side, the occasional indulgence became a testament to the progress made rather than a return to the past. Avani's understanding and unwavering support turned what seemed like an insurmountable mountain into a conquerable hill, making each step toward a healthier lifestyle a shared victory in our evolving journey together.

Our love story took on an enchanting dimension with Avani's deep affection for cats. This shared appreciation became a delightful ritual, a charming adventure that unfolded at a quaint tea shop nestled in the heart of the city.

The anticipation of our visits added a sweet touch to our routine. Arriving on my bike, I would eagerly wait at Avani's hostel, the minutes stretching like delicate threads woven into the fabric of our shared moments. When she emerged, our journey to the tea shop became more than just a physical traversal; it was a celebration of togetherness.

As we approached the tea shop, the familiar sight of a cute, white, fluffy cat greeted us. Its playful demeanor and gentle purrs formed the soundtrack to our shared escapades. The tea shop, once a simple venue, transformed into a haven where the aroma of brewing tea intertwined with the warmth of our connection.

Seated at a cozy corner, surrounded by the comforting ambiance, our conversations meandered effortlessly. The cat, a silent witness to our unfolding romance, added a touch of whimsy to our exchanges. Moments of shared laughter and the exchange of affectionate glances became the essence of those visits.

In the tapestry of our love story, these tea shop escapades were like intricately embroidered patches—each visit adding a layer of sweetness to our narrative. The journey, from Avani's hostel to the tea shop and back, became a cherished routine, a canvas painted with the hues of shared laughter, subtle gestures, and the joy of simple pleasures.

What began as a cute exploration of a shared interest in cats evolved into a cherished tradition. The tea shop, with its fluffy feline resident, became a place where the ordinary turned extraordinary, and every cup of tea held the warmth of our affection.

The extension of our love for cats found a tangible expression in the form of multiple feline companions that adorned Avani's home. Our shared visits to the local pet doctor became not just a routine but a delightful adventure, a way to ensure the well-being of our fluffy friends.

Accompanied by the comforting hum of my bike, we embarked on these excursions to the pet doctor, our shared commitment to the welfare of Avani's cats creating a bond that extended beyond our own relationship. The pet clinic, with its familiar scent of antiseptic and the comforting presence of various pets, became a familiar backdrop to our shared endeavors.

Navigating the aisles of the pet store, we carefully selected not just cat medicine but also an array of treats and toys, each chosen with the intention of adding joy to our feline companions' lives. The process of deciding on the perfect cat food and supplements became a collaborative effort, mirroring the harmony and synergy within our relationship.

Back at Avani's home, she usually use to spend quality time with the cats, their playful antics and purrs creating a soothing melody in the background. The routine visits to the pet doctor and the shared responsibility of caring for her cats not only strengthened our bond but also nurtured a sense of shared responsibility and commitment.

In the world of veterinary clinics and aisles of cat supplies, we discovered not just a routine but a shared passion. These moments became threads intricately woven into the tapestry of our relationship, a testament to the depth of our connection and the shared love that extended to every member, furry or otherwise, in our shared world.

As the curtain drew close on the second year, our shared journey unfolded like a tapestry woven with threads of love, laughter, and shared adventures. The routine visits to the tea shop, the comforting presence of cats, and the collaborative efforts in caring for them became the defining moments of our evolving relationship.

Approaching the end of the academic year, everything seemed to align in a symphony of joy and contentment. The challenges we overcame, the shared laughter echoing through the corridors of our college, and the countless small moments that shaped our narrative were now etched into the pages of our shared history.

The city of Jaipur, once an unfamiliar terrain, had become a backdrop to our love story, and the transition from the college hostel to independent living became a testament to the growth and resilience of our connection. As we stood on the threshold of a new chapter, the sense of fulfillment and anticipation lingered in the air, promising that the forthcoming chapters would be just as enchanting as those that unfolded in the second year of our shared collegiate tale.

CHAPTER TWELVE

RADIANT HORIZONS: EMBRACING JOY BEYOND

Entering the threshold of the third year, joy permeated the very essence of our days. The vibrant tapestry of our college life seemed to be painted with hues of celebration, marking the pinnacle of our shared happiness. The anticipation of a new chapter unfolded against the backdrop of camaraderie, laughter, and the promise of unforgettable moments.

Our college life became a mosaic of celebration, with parties and gatherings dotting the landscape of our routine. Every corner echoed with the symphony of shared laughter, a testament to the strong bonds we had forged. The camaraderie among friends, the sense of achievement in our academic pursuits, and the underlying current of happiness painted a picture of fulfillment and contentment.

As we embraced the rhythm of the third year, the joy that enveloped us extended beyond the classrooms. The pulse of our shared adventures quickened, and every outing became a celebration of the extraordinary within the ordinary. The city of Jaipur, with its myriad attractions, became a playground for our exploration, and each trip held the promise of new discoveries.

In the midst of this jubilation, a significant shift unfolded as Avani emerged from the confines of the hostel and embraced a new phase of independence. The decision to step outside the hostel walls marked not only a change in living arrangements but also symbolized the blossoming of newfound freedom and autonomy.

Our shared experiences, from the lively parties to the explorations of the city's hidden gems, fortified the bonds that held our collective joy together. The third year, like a chapter in a delightful novel, commenced with an exuberant celebration of life, love, and the unwavering connection that defined the essence of our shared journey.

Embarking on a journey that transcended the confines of our college walls, we found ourselves immersed in the excitement of planning an outing with one of Avani's close friend and her boyfriend. The destination was no ordinary spot—it was the enchanting city of Jaisalmer, a place I had dreamt of visiting since childhood. The prospect of experiencing the vast desert landscapes was not just a trip; it was the realization of a cherished dream.

Our adventure began with the meticulous planning of a trip package. It included individual sleeper coaches for each couple, ensuring a comfortable and private journey. As the wheels of the bus began to roll, the anticipation bubbled within us. We settled into our cozy sleeper compartments, peering out of the windows at the ever-changing scenery, counting animals along the way, and creating memories that would linger long after the journey's end.

Upon our arrival in Jaisalmer, we were warmly welcomed by our trip adviser, who ushered us to a charming hotel where we could freshen up and prepare for the adventures that awaited. The air was filled with an eagerness to explore, and the prospect of discovering the hidden gems of Jaisalmer added an extra layer of excitement.

Our first day in the city commenced with a guided tour of Jaisalmer, an ancient city steeped in history and adorned with intricately carved architecture. Every corner unfolded a story, and the golden hues of the sandstone structures seemed to narrate tales of a bygone era. From the majestic Jaisalmer Fort to the narrow lanes of the old city, each step was a dance with history, and every glance exchanged between us spoke volumes about the joy of shared exploration.

As the sun dipped below the horizon, casting a warm golden glow over the city of Jaisalmer, our journey took an exciting turn. The evening found us at the mesmerizing Sam Sand Dunes, where the promise of an authentic desert experience unfolded. The anticipation heightened as we were assigned individual tents, each one a cozy sanctuary beneath the expansive canvas of the desert sky.

Our tents, adorned with vibrant fabrics and rustic charm, offered a perfect blend of comfort and adventure. The gentle rustle of the desert wind and the soft glow of lanterns set the stage for an enchanting night ahead. The atmosphere was filled with an air of anticipation, and the flickering flames of the campfire beckoned us to gather around.

As the evening unfolded, we were treated to a panoramic view of the desert stretching endlessly in every direction. The shifting sands painted a mesmerizing landscape, a tranquil canvas illuminated by the warm hues of twilight. The sense of awe and wonder enveloped us as we stood on the dunes, the vastness of the desert captivating our hearts.

The night took an adventurous turn with a thrilling jeep safari through the undulating sand dunes. The adrenaline surged as the jeeps navigated the challenging terrain, creating waves of excitement among us. The moonlit desert, with its mystical allure, became the backdrop to a ride filled with laughter, shouts of joy, and the sheer exhilaration of the moment.

Returning to the campsite, we were treated to a cultural extravaganza—a vibrant display of folk dances and traditional music. The rhythmic beats reverberated through the desert, and the performers, adorned in colorful attire, transported us to a world of ancient tales and timeless traditions. The cultural immersion continued with a delectable spread of local dishes served under the starlit sky, creating a sensory journey that fused taste with the essence of the desert.

As the night unfolded, we retreated to our tents for a cozy sleep under the desert stars. The tranquility of the surroundings and the distant whispers of the night created an ambiance of serene intimacy, making our desert encampment a haven of shared moments and shared dreams.

The next morning brought a new adventure—a long camel ride into the heart of the desert, leading us towards the Indo-Pak border. The vast, lonely expanse of the desert revealed itself, with only our caravan of camels breaking the stillness. The profound sense of solitude became a backdrop to shared conversations, laughter, and the unspoken bonds that deepened in the quietude of the desert.

After the camel ride, our group gathered for talks and games in the midst of the dunes. The laughter echoed against the vastness, creating memories that resonated in the endless landscape. As the sun began its descent, painting the sky with hues of orange and pink, we settled into the sands, embracing the simplicity of shared moments and the timeless beauty of the desert.

The night was filled with more laughter, camaraderie, and a sense of togetherness. The flickering flames of a bonfire cast dancing shadows on the sands, creating a warm and intimate atmosphere. With stories shared, games played, and the distant silhouette of the dunes against the night sky, we drifted into sleep, the desert cradling us in its tranquil embrace.

Our return journey brought a thrilling climax to our desert adventure. Squad biking and paragliding added an exhilarating touch to our trip, providing an adrenaline rush that complemented the serene moments we had experienced in the desert. Returning to the city of Jaipur, our hearts brimming with memories and laughter, we realized that the Jaisalmer trip wasn't just an excursion; it was a tapestry woven with threads of joy, adventure, and the enduring bonds of friendship and love. It stood as a testament to the magic that unfolds when dreams are realized in the vast expanses of the desert, under the starlit skies that bear witness to the stories of those who dare to explore.

Indeed, the magic of the Jaisalmer trip wasn't solely woven into the intricate tapestry of desert landscapes, cultural performances, and thrilling adventures. The true enchantment lay in the presence of Avani, the one who turned every moment into a treasure and every experience into a shared adventure. In the vastness of the desert and the laughter under the starlit sky, our connection deepened, and the journey became more than just a travel escapade—it became a celebration of togetherness.

The radiance of Avani's laughter echoed against the sand dunes, creating a melody that harmonized with the rustling winds of the desert. As we explored the untouched beauty of Jaisalmer, her presence became the compass that guided us through the labyrinth of experiences. Every shared glance, every shared laughter, and every shared silence added a layer of richness to the memories we were crafting in the golden embrace of the desert.

Whether it was the warmth of the campfire, the thrill of the jeep safari, or the serenity of the camel ride, Avani's presence transformed these moments into something extraordinary. The laughter that resonated in the desert night was a testament to the joy we found in each other's company, turning a remarkable trip into an unforgettable chapter in the story of us.

As we returned to the bustling city lights of Jaipur, the realization dawned that the true essence of the journey wasn't merely the places we visited or the adventures we undertook; it was the companionship that turned those moments into lasting memories. With Avani by my side, every experience became an exploration of shared joy, and every destination became a backdrop to the evolving narrative of our love story. Indeed, the Jaisalmer trip was not just the best because of the places we visited, but because I was fortunate enough to traverse the golden sands of the desert with Avani, turning every grain into a treasure trove of shared happiness.

Throughout the entirety of our third year, the essence of adventure extended beyond the mesmerizing landscapes of Jaisalmer. Biking became more than just a mode of transportation; it became a metaphor for the journey we were navigating together. The open roads, wind in our hair, and the hum of the engine formed the backdrop to a plethora of new experiences.

The roar of the motorcycle engine echoed the highs and lows of our journey. There were moments of exhilaration as we explored new terrains, discovering hidden gems and creating memories along winding roads. Each bend held the promise of a new adventure, and the thrill of the ride mirrored the unpredictability of life itself.

Yet, as with any journey, there were also challenges and occasional bumps in the road. The ups and downs, whether metaphorical or on the asphalt, were met with resilience and a shared determination to overcome them. It was during these moments that Avani's unwavering support became a stabilizing force, turning challenges into opportunities for growth and strengthening the bond that held us together.

The open road became a canvas for shared dreams, conversations that spanned the miles, and the forging of a connection that withstood the twists and turns of life. The biking escapades weren't just about reaching destinations; they were about the journey itself, where every experience, every shared laughter, and every silent contemplation on the road became a stroke on the canvas of our evolving relationship.

As the final pages of the third-year chapter unfolded, the narrative of our journey bore witness to a profound realization—one that echoed in the quiet moments, the laughter shared under desert skies, and the hum of the motorcycle engines. It was a realization that crystallized in the very essence of Avani's presence in my life.

Avani wasn't just a companion on the adventures of Jaisalmer or the winding roads we traversed on our bikes; she was the heart and soul of a journey that unfolded beyond the physical landscapes. Her laughter echoed against the sand dunes, her presence added a special warmth to the flickering flames of the campfire, and her unwavering support became the anchor in the highs and lows of our shared experiences.

The open roads, the vast desert horizons, and the shared moments of joy painted a portrait of a woman who, in every sense, seemed tailor-made for the chapters of my life. Her spirit was a force of nature, mirroring the winds that whispered through the dunes and the resilience of the desert that bloomed under the harsh sun. Avani wasn't just a passenger in the journey; she was the co-author of the story, contributing nuances, depth, and color to the narrative.

In the hustle and bustle of college life, the challenges faced, and the exhilaration of new experiences, Avani remained a constant, a source of strength and joy. Her ability to find joy in the simplest of moments, to embrace challenges with grace, and to share in the triumphs and tribulations of life painted her as not just a companion but a life partner in the making.

The biking escapades were a metaphor for our relationship—navigating the twists and turns with shared excitement, resilience, and a sense of mutual exploration. As we clocked miles and created memories on the road, it became increasingly evident that Avani was more than a co-pilot; she was the navigator of my heart, leading us toward a destination that felt like home.

As the year drew to a close, a profound certainty settled within me—a certainty that Avani was not just someone I wanted to share my life with, but the person I couldn't imagine my life without. The laughter that echoed, the adventures that unfolded, and the quiet moments of shared understanding all pointed to a profound truth—she was made for me, and I for her.

With the turning of each page in the book of our shared experiences, the narrative became more intricate, more colorful, and undeniably more beautiful. Avani's laughter was the melody that accompanied our journey, her presence the beacon guiding us through uncharted territories. The resilience and strength she exhibited in the face of challenges became a testament to the unwavering bond we had cultivated.

In the quiet reflections of the year, as we gazed at the starlit skies of the desert or cruised through the night on our bikes, the realization crystallized. I never wanted to lose her. Avani wasn't just a chapter in the story of my life; she was the story—a story of love, resilience, shared dreams, and the unspoken understanding that made each day a celebration.

And so, as the third year drew to an end, I stood at the threshold of a future that seemed brighter, more enchanting, and undoubtedly shared with the person who had become the soulmate of my journey. The pages of the third-year chapter held not just the tales of our adventures but also the assurance that, in Avani, I had found the one who made the journey worthwhile, and with whom I wanted to script countless chapters in the book of a lifetime together.

CHAPTER THIRTEEN

WHISPERS OF TRUST: ECHOES OF FAREWELL

The opening verses of the final year unfolded like the first notes of a poignant symphony, reverberating through the corridors of academia with the rhythm of endings and beginnings. The atmosphere buzzed with a palpable energy, a fusion of excitement and nostalgia as students embarked on the culmination of their college journey. It was against this backdrop of mixed emotions that Avani and I entered the final act of our shared narrative.

The academic corridors, once familiar yet now tinged with a sense of wistfulness, bore witness to the dawn of our senior year. As the days unfolded, the promise of placements hung in the air, bringing with it the prospect of charting new courses beyond the walls that had shaped our college experiences. The hallways echoed with conversations about career paths, ambitions, and the subtle undercurrents of trust that began to weave through the fabric of our relationship.

In the initial moments, there was a palpable lightness, an air of camaraderie that transcended the confines of lecture halls and spilled into shared laughter in cafeterias. Avani and I, like fellow protagonists in a familiar tale, navigated the intricacies of trust with a newfound understanding. The barriers, once guarded, began to soften, allowing the vulnerabilities beneath to emerge.

Placements became more than just professional prospects; they became the crucible in which the elements of trust, uncertainty, and the impending farewell converged. Avani's trust in me deepened, each shared conversation and mutual support fostering a connection that hinted at the profound bond we had built over the years.

As the sun cast its first rays over the horizon, signaling the beginning of a new academic year, Avani took a leap into a new phase of our relationship—she moved in with me. The modest apartment, once solitary, now echoed with the laughter and warmth of shared moments. Avani, with her infectious enthusiasm, brought a new vibrancy to our living space.

In the heart of our home, the kitchen, Avani transformed mundane ingredients into culinary symphonies. The aroma of her creations wafted through the air, an invitation to the feast of shared meals and intimate conversations. Her culinary skills became not just a delight for the taste buds but a tangible expression of the care and attention she poured into our life together.

Days seamlessly blended into nights as we embraced the rhythm of living together 24/7. The walls of our abode absorbed the echoes of our laughter, the hushed tones of late-night conversations, and the whispers of dreams shared in the stillness of the night. Our shared space became a canvas where the brushstrokes of daily life painted a portrait of togetherness, a masterpiece in the making.

In the realm of academia, the 7th-semester exams loomed on the horizon, casting a shadow of anticipation and determination. Our study sessions turned into collaborative endeavors, where the weight of textbooks was lightened by shared insights and mutual support. The very act of studying together became a testament to the strength of our connection—a synergy that transcended the academic challenges we faced.

Amid the hushed rustle of turning pages and the soft glow of study lamps, we created a cocoon of shared ambitions and collective aspirations. The days leading up to the exams were marked not only by the pursuit of academic excellence but also by the joy of navigating the challenges hand in hand.

As the exam days unfolded, the tension in the air was met with a calm assurance born out of our shared preparation. Avani's presence, like a reassuring anchor, provided a sense of stability in the face of academic uncertainties. Together, we weathered the storms of exam stress, emerging on the other side with a sense of accomplishment and the knowledge that our partnership was a source of strength.

The 7th semester exams became more than a measure of academic proficiency; they became a testament to the resilience of our relationship. With each successfully tackled exam paper, we added another layer to the tapestry of shared victories, reinforcing the belief that together, we could overcome any challenge.

As the final exam papers were submitted, a sense of accomplishment washed over us, and we reveled in the shared triumph. The journey through the 7th semester had not only fortified our academic pursuits but also deepened the bonds of companionship. With the scent of academic success lingering in the air and the echoes of shared laughter resonating in our hearts, we stood on the precipice of a new chapter, ready to face whatever lay ahead.

In the wake of our triumph in the 7th-semester exams, the next chapter unfolded with the onset of placement season. As the corridors of anticipation echoed with footsteps of uncertainty, a unique blend of excitement and anxiety permeated the air. The dance of possibilities commenced, and the very first notes of this professional overture played out in the field of artificial intelligence development.

A serendipitous turn of fate led me to the doorstep of the very first company, beckoning me into the realm of cutting-edge artificial intelligence. The offer extended its hand, and I grasped it, stepping into a world where algorithms and innovation wove the fabric of tomorrow's technology.

While my path found a promising direction, a collective pulse of concern echoed among my peers. The question lingered in the air like an unresolved chord: What lay ahead for them? The weight of uncertainty bore down on many, painting the scene with hues of stress and anticipation.

As colleagues navigated the tumultuous sea of interviews and selection processes, the spectrum of emotions varied from hope to trepidation. Each handshake with a potential employer became a step on the tightrope of professional destiny, and the corridors whispered with the shared heartbeat of aspiring individuals seeking their place in the professional landscape.

In the midst of this dynamic panorama, the very first notes of my professional journey were struck. The canvas of artificial intelligence development unfolded before me, and I embarked on a journey where innovation and creativity were the brushstrokes shaping the technological landscape of the future.

As the spotlight of opportunity focused on me, the shadows of concern and doubt played out in the collective psyche of my peers. The uncertainties of the professional world cast their long shadows, but the resilience and spirit of exploration prevailed. Together, we faced the unknown, aware that the road ahead was an uncharted territory filled with both challenges and triumphs.

The placement season became more than a series of job interviews; it became a crucible of shared experiences, a collective narrative of dreams taking flight and the resilience to face the unknown. The corridors, once resonating with academic discussions, transformed into a stage where professional aspirations took center stage.

In this symphony of transition, the first company's embrace of artificial intelligence development marked not only a personal victory but also a chapter in the evolving story of our professional journeys. As the curtains rose on the placement season, the script of the future remained unwritten, and each individual, with dreams in their eyes, awaited their turn on the stage of professional possibilities.

The decision to accept the first offer, while not the most lucrative in terms of financial compensation, carried with it the promise of invaluable experience in a reputable setting. As I took the plunge into the realms of artificial intelligence development, the anticipation of learning and growth overshadowed the considerations of a hefty package.

However, the commitment to the initial offer came with a trade-off. Having accepted the position, the door to further interviews and potential opportunities closed, limiting my ability to explore alternative professional avenues. The choice to dive headfirst into this particular venture was a testament to the belief in the value of experience and the prospect of honing skills in a prestigious environment.

Amidst this professional journey, fate took another turn as Avani, after a month of anticipation and pursuit, secured a position in a renowned multinational corporation. The offer not only brought with it the prestige of a reputable organization but also a financial package that reflected the recognition of her skills and expertise.

The diverging paths in our professional narratives became evident. While my journey started with the exploration of artificial intelligence in a setting rich with learning opportunities, Avani's trajectory soared with a placement in a high-profile multinational company.

The dynamics of our individual pursuits underscored the unpredictable nature of the professional landscape. As I delved into the realms of AI development, Avani charted her course in the echelons of corporate success as a software developer. The symphony of our careers played out in contrasting notes, each contributing to the rich tapestry of our shared experiences.

The juxtaposition of these divergent professional arcs set the stage for new challenges and milestones, and as we navigated the intricate dance of career trajectories, the shared anticipation of the unknown future brought an element of excitement to our evolving narrative.

In the intricate dance of our professional journeys, the contrast between my startup venture and Avani's position in a multinational corporation painted the canvas of our careers with diverse hues. Our emotions swayed between happiness and a tinge of sadness, echoing the complex melody of embarking on separate paths.

The startup environment offered me the promise of innovation, flexibility, and the thrill of contributing to the growth of a nascent venture. Despite the modest beginnings, there was an underlying excitement in being part of a team that sought to carve its niche in the industry. The prospect of learning and shaping the trajectory of a budding company brought a sense of fulfillment.

On the other hand, Avani's position in a multinational corporation symbolized stability, established systems, and the prestige that came with being associated with a renowned entity. The allure of global opportunities and the structured corporate environment offered a different set of experiences, bringing with it the weight of corporate legacy and the promise of a well-charted career path.

The happiness of securing meaningful opportunities was interwoven with a hint of sadness as the geographical distance between our workplaces meant navigating a period of separation. The realization that our professional paths led us to different locations brought a bittersweet undertone to the excitement.

Yet, time stood as our ally. A window of six months unfolded before us—a precious span to savor the present, plan for the future, and make the most of the moments we shared. The looming commencement of our work added a ticking clock to our shared timeline, urging us to embrace the opportunities that lay ahead and make the most of the time we had together.

The unique blend of emotions—happiness for our respective successes, sadness for the distance that lay ahead, and anticipation for the journey ahead—set the stage for a chapter that held the promise of growth, new experiences, and the resilience of our bond. As we stood on the precipice of a significant juncture in our lives, the countdown to the beginning of our professional endeavors echoed with the harmonies of change and the melody of shared aspirations.

As the symphony of our professional trajectories played its final notes, we found ourselves standing at the crossroads of divergence and anticipation. The canvas of our careers had been painted with contrasting strokes—innovation and flexibility in the startup realm, juxtaposed against the stability and global allure of a multinational corporation. The emotions that swirled within us, a blend of happiness and a hint of melancholy, mirrored the intricacies of our evolving narrative.

The startup landscape offered the thrill of the unknown, a promise to contribute to something burgeoning with potential. It was an exhilarating journey into uncharted territories, where every challenge became an opportunity to shape the destiny of a nascent venture. On the flip side, Avani's position in a multinational corporation carried the weight of established systems, the prestige of corporate legacy, and the allure of a well-defined career path.

As we grappled with the geographical separation that our professional choices entailed, the ticking clock of the looming work commencement underscored the transient nature of our shared moments. The forthcoming six months emerged as a temporal haven—a window to savor the present, plan for the future, and revel in the shared joys that awaited us.

In the somber unfolding of events, a disheartening revelation cast its shadow upon my professional endeavors—a lamentable message arrived, announcing the closure of the very company that had extended its employ to me. Stranded in the aftermath of this unfortunate occurrence, the tendrils of unemployment wound their way around my aspirations. Yet, in the face of this adversity, I chose not to unveil the depths of my despondency to her, opting for a stoic facade to shield against the gravity of the situation.

Resolute and composed, I refrained from wearing my distress overtly, choosing a veneer of confidence as my armor. It was a conscious decision, a calculated effort to spare her the anguish that mirrored the bleakness of my professional landscape. While the weight of joblessness burdened my shoulders, I bore it with a semblance of assurance, convincing myself that resilience would be my guiding light through this unforeseen darkness.

As the sands of time continued their unrelenting march, the crucible of our academic journey culminated in the crucible of the final exams. In defiance of the tumultuous circumstances, we rose to the occasion, exhibiting a prowess that belied the turbulence in my professional realm. The echoes of success reverberated through our accomplishments, creating a harmonious counterpoint to the dissonance of unemployment.

In retrospect, the juxtaposition of personal and academic triumph against the backdrop of professional adversity painted a tableau of resilience—a testament to the fortitude that emerged from the crucible of challenges.

The curtain fell on this chapter, leaving us with a bittersweet anticipation of the journey ahead. The unique blend of emotions, the harmonies of change, and the melody of shared aspirations set the stage for a promising yet challenging adventure. The countdown to the beginning of our professional endeavors echoed the cadence of transition, urging us to step boldly into the unknown. Together, we embraced the promise of growth, new experiences, and the enduring resilience of our bond, ready to script the next chapter of our intertwined narratives.

CHAPTER FOURTEEN

Echoes of Departure: Navigating the Goodbye

After the finals, Avani and I decided to seize the opportunity to create lasting memories. The focal point of our plans centered around an intimate journey, just the two of us, to the enchanting destinations of Pushkar and Ajmer.

As the anticipation of our upcoming roles simmered in the background, we embarked on a journey that promised not only scenic landscapes but also moments of shared serenity. Pushkar, with its mystical aura and tranquil lakes, beckoned us to explore its timeless beauty. Ajmer, steeped in history and spirituality, stood as a testament to the cultural richness of the region.

The trip, meticulously planned to embrace the essence of both locations, to became a metaphorical bookmark in our shared narrative. It symbolized not only a pause before the professional crescendo but also an ode to the quietude that we cherished in each other's company.

The journey to Pushkar marked the commencement of our intimate getaway, an escape into the realms of tranquility and natural beauty. The chosen resort, a mesmerizing enclave tucked away from the hustle and bustle, unfolded before us like a hidden gem waiting to be discovered. After a well-deserved rest, we awakened to the promise of exploration.

Opting for a ride we embraced the freedom of charting our course through the enchanting landscapes of Pushkar. The winding roads led us to the heart of this mystical town, where every corner held the allure of discovery.

As the wheels rolled along, Pushkar unfolded its secrets—the vibrant markets adorned with colorful textiles and handicrafts, the aromatic wafts from street food stalls enticing our taste buds, and the echoes of spiritual chants resonating through the air. The sacred Pushkar Lake, a central point of serenity, mirrored the azure sky, inviting us to immerse ourselves in its timeless beauty.

We strolled through the narrow lanes, embraced by the charm of ancient temples and the lively energy of the local markets. The vibrant hues of Pushkar became a palette of shared experiences, painting our journey with memories that transcended the ordinary.

It became dream of exploration, navigating the intricate tapestry of Pushkar's culture and traditions. From the panoramic views atop Ratnagiri Hill to the vibrant spectacle of the Brahma Temple, each destination added a layer to our shared adventure.

As the day unfolded, we found ourselves drawn to the cultural fusion that Pushkar offered. The evening brought a serene calmness, and we basked in the ambiance of the resort, reflecting on the kaleidoscope of experiences that had colored our day.

We were carrying our soul through the landscapes of discovery and connecting the dots of our journey. The beauty of Pushkar, discovered hand in hand, laid the foundation for the memories we would carry forward into the chapters of our shared history.

The culmination of a day filled with exploration and shared moments brought us back to the comforting embrace of the resort. The weariness from our adventures was met with the soothing promise of a refreshing bath, cleansing away the remnants of the day's journey.

As the water cascaded, we exchanged stories and reflections, the bathroom becoming a sanctuary for shared laughter and quiet contemplation. The day's experiences lingered in the air, intertwined with the warmth of the resort, creating a cocoon of serenity that enveloped us.

Dinner became a continuation of the day's culinary discoveries. The resort, with its culinary delights, served as the backdrop for a meal that mirrored the richness of Pushkar's flavors. The shared table became a space for not just savoring delicacies but also relishing the camaraderie that defined our journey.

With satisfied appetites and content hearts, we retreated to the haven of our room. The quietude of the night wrapped around us like a gentle lullaby, easing us into a restful slumber. The day's memories, imprinted in the tapestry of our shared experiences, accompanied us into the realm of dreams.

Under the veil of night, Pushkar's magic continued to weave its spell, and we surrendered to the embrace of sleep, anticipating the dawn that would usher in another day of exploration and connection. As the curtains fell on this chapter of our journey, the dreams that danced on the horizon hinted at the promise of more adventures awaiting us in the enchanting landscapes of Pushkar.

The dawn of the next day heralded a continuation of our journey as we embarked on the road from Pushkar to the historic city of Ajmer. The self-driving cab became our chariot once again, weaving through the scenic landscapes that connected these two gems of Rajasthan.

As we entered Ajmer, the tapestry of history unfolded before us—a rich mosaic of architecture, spirituality, and cultural resonance. The ancient alleys bore witness to the ebb and flow of time, inviting us to explore every nook and cranny of this enchanting city.

Our first stop led us to the serene Ana Sagar Lake, where the gentle ripples mirrored the timeless tranquility of the surroundings. The allure of boating beckoned, and we found ourselves gliding across the mirrored surface, surrounded by the panoramic views of Ajmer's architectural wonders.

The boat became our vessel of joy, ferrying us through the reflections of the Dargah Sharif and the surrounding ghats. The laughter echoed over the water, mingling with the cultural resonance of the city. The joy of exploration was encapsulated in each stroke of the oar and the shared gaze across the shimmering expanse.

Exploring Ajmer took us through the heart of its heritage—the majestic Ajmer Sharif Dargah, the regal beauty of the Taragarh Fort, and the architectural marvels of the Adhai Din Ka Jhonpra. Each site offered a glimpse into the layers of history that had shaped this city, leaving an indelible mark on the fabric of our shared memories.

The vibrant bazaars of Ajmer, with their kaleidoscope of colors and aromas, added a touch of local flavor to our exploration. Sampling street food delicacies and immersing ourselves in the bustling market scenes became a celebration of Ajmer's cultural vibrancy.

As the day unfolded, we discovered the hidden corners and lesser-known gems of Ajmer, relishing the magic that this city held. The self-driving cab transformed into a time-traveling companion, transporting us through the ages and connecting us to the soul of Ajmer.

The evening set against the backdrop of the setting sun found us at the serene Pushkar Lake, where the rhythmic chants and the tranquility of the surroundings offered a serene farewell to our exploration. The memories created during our exploration of Ajmer would forever remain etched in the canvas of our shared experiences, a testament to the magic that unfolded in the heart of Rajasthan.

After our enriching exploration of Ajmer, we returned to the comforting haven of our cozy resort in Pushkar. The setting sun painted the skies with hues of warm orange and pink, casting a tranquil glow over the landscape. The promise of serene evenings and shared moments beckoned as we prepared to uncover the remaining hidden gems of Pushkar.

Venturing into the lesser-known corners of Pushkar, we discovered pockets of tranquility that resonated with the town's mystique. Each step brought us closer to the heart of Pushkar's cultural tapestry, weaving together the threads of history, spirituality, and the unexplored.

Amidst the labyrinthine lanes, we encountered artisanal workshops, vibrant markets, and charming cafes tucked away from the bustling crowds. Pushkar, with its eclectic mix of traditions and contemporary allure, unfolded before us like a story waiting to be read in its entirety.

Our days were adorned with visits to sacred temples, serene ghats, and viewpoints that offered panoramic vistas of the town. The melodies of temple bells, the aromatic swirl of incense, and the gentle whispers of the wind created a symphony that echoed the timeless charm of Pushkar.

As we explored the town's nooks and crannies, each encounter became a verse in the ballad of our shared journey. From the intricately adorned Brahma Temple to the spiritual ambiance of Varaha Ghat, Pushkar unveiled its treasures, and we reveled in the magic that lingered in every corner.

With every step, we were not just exploring Pushkar; we were immersing ourselves in the narratives etched into its ancient walls. The shared laughter, the quiet contemplation, and the unspoken understanding deepened the bonds that connected us to this sacred town.

The days unfolded seamlessly, filled with moments that transcended the ordinary. Whether it was a leisurely stroll around Pushkar Lake or savoring local delicacies in hidden eateries, each experience became a brushstroke in the portrait of our final days in this enchanting realm.

The serene nights in Pushkar held a subtle undercurrent of change, a shift that disrupted the tranquility we had grown accustomed to. On one particular night, a restlessness lingered in the air, awakening me from the depths of slumber. There, in the soft glow of moonlight, Avani appeared engrossed in a conversation, her eagerness palpable as she fervently dialed a number.

The hushed murmurs and the urgency in her voice hinted at a conversation laden with significance. Intrigued yet choosing not to pry, I chose to overlook the peculiar night's events, drifting back into a realm of dreams. Little did I fathom that this seemingly ordinary moment held the whispers of change, silently echoing the impending shift in the tides of our shared narrative.

The inadvertent awakening in the silent hours of the night unraveled a sequence of events that would cast a shadow over the tranquility we had known. Sensing an underlying unease, I mustered the courage to share my feelings of discomfort with Avani. However, she dismissed my concerns, claiming to have drifted into a deep slumber.

Driven by a curiosity that bordered on anxiety, I found myself glancing at her phone, a subtle act that would expose the fracture in our trust. The call logs revealed a series of conversations with a friend, a name that had once been a mere presence on the periphery of our lives. However, this friend had harbored resentment, issuing challenges to our relationship and expressing a desire to disrupt our happiness.

A surge of conflicting emotions engulfed me as I discovered the intensity of their recent interactions, particularly on a night where my discomfort had been dismissed. The revelation pierced through the foundations of trust, leaving behind a sense of betrayal. Avani's choice to conceal the extent of her conversations with this friend, coupled with his explicit intentions to undermine our relationship, became a poignant fissure that shattered the semblance of security we had built together. The fragility of trust, once broken, laid bare the vulnerability of our connection, leaving me grappling with the profound impact of that night's revelations.

In the wake of the night's revelations, I gathered the remnants of courage and delicately broached the subject with Avani the following day. With a heavy heart, I inquired about her continued communication with the friend whose intentions had cast a looming shadow over our once-shared sanctuary. Her response, a simple "NO," hung in the air, a stark contrast to the intricate web of interactions that unfolded on her phone.

In that vulnerable moment, I bared my wounded heart, confessing that I had glimpsed into the clandestine conversations that had unfolded in the silent hours of the night. Tears, both silent and shared, became the medium through which our unspoken pain manifested. Confronting the betrayal that had taken refuge in the shadows, we reached a somber consensus – to end our shared journey, drawing a painful conclusion to the chapter that held the echoes of Pushkar's enchantment.

The decision to part ways in the midst of our trip became an unspoken acknowledgment of the irreparable damage inflicted upon the foundations of our connection. Avani, choosing to return to her home in Jaipur, and I, retreating to the solitude of our apartment, navigated the physical and emotional distance that now loomed between us. The remnants of shared dreams, laughter, and the magic of Pushkar were overshadowed by the weight of decisions made and trust shattered. And so, in the aftermath of that fateful night, the threads that had once woven our stories together began to unravel, each step marking a painful descent from the heights of shared euphoria to the depths of separation.

The parting at the familiar roundabout near her home carried with it the weight of unspoken goodbyes. A forced smile adorned her face, a fleeting moment etched in the frame of a photograph. As I retraced my steps to the quiet solitude of my room, the emptiness echoed the silent reverberations of a goodbye too painful to articulate.

Yearning for a connection severed by distance, I reached out through the digital realm, the dial tone punctuating the solitude. The call remained unanswered, a palpable silence bridging the physical gap that now stretched between us. In the quiet corners of my room, the ache of loneliness and the haunting specter of what was lost settled, enveloping me in the melancholy of unspoken farewells. A poignant reminder that in the void left by departure, the echoes of connection persist, resonating in the unattended calls and the silence that follows.

The abrupt turn of events brought an unexpected wave of sorrow crashing into the fragile sanctuary of my life. The news of a sudden death summoned me back to the familiar confines of home, where the air hung heavy with grief. Yet, as I unpacked the weight of one loss, another cruel blow awaited—an additional departure that deepened the chasm of despair within me.

Navigating the disorienting whirlwind of emotions, I sought solace in the one connection that had once been a source of comfort. Desperate for understanding, I reached out to her, hoping for a lifeline amidst the tumultuous sea of grief. However, the echoing silence on the other end of the line only amplified the isolation, leaving me to grapple with the weight of loss and the unsettling turbulence of unaddressed pain.

As the days blurred into months, the shadows of brokenness and depression grew more pronounced. She, too, embarked on a new chapter, relocating to Bangalore for a fresh start. Unfamiliar with the intricacies of her evolving life, I found myself drowning in the silence, a solitary figure grappling with the complexities of grief and a journey that had become an isolating odyssey.

In the midst of my own shattered world, the lack of support and understanding deepened the abyss of despair. The once-shared dreams now lay fragmented, and the semblance of a future had become an elusive mirage. The narrative that unfolded was one of profound loss, a tapestry woven with threads of heartache and an overwhelming sense of solitude that echoed in the void left by her absence.

The unfolding chapters of life brought me to a crossroads where the weight of unemployment and depression converged in a perfect storm. In this crucible of personal challenges, the need for her presence became an anchor in the tempest of uncertainty. Yet, it was precisely at this juncture—the most unfortunate time—that she chose to part ways, leaving me to grapple with the intricacies of my own struggles.

The timing, cruel and unforgiving, amplified the intensity of the emotional tempest. Unemployment and the shadows of depression cast long shadows over the landscape of my life, and the absence of her support became an additional burden to bear. It was a poignant intersection of vulnerability and loss, where the need for solace collided with the stark reality of solitude.

In the tapestry of personal challenges, this moment stood out as a testament to the unpredictable nature of life's trials—a convergence of adversity when support was most sought. The narrative unfolded with a bitter undertone, painting a portrait of resilience tested at the very precipice of despair.

In the desolate tapestry of our unraveling connection, I pleaded with her, each request a desperate cry in the vast emptiness that had engulfed us. "Come back, even if just for a moment," I implored, hoping that the echo of my words might resonate through the walls she had erected. My pleas, borne of raw vulnerability, met her gaze but failed to pierce the barriers she had constructed. In the silent transaction of emotions, my entreaties were cast as selfish, a bitter label that clung to the core of my desperation.

The labyrinth of unanswered questions loomed large, veiled in the obscurity of undisclosed reasons. What invisible forces had conspired to steer our shared journey into the tumultuous tempest, I could only speculate. The quest for understanding, a beacon in the storm, found no refuge in her silence. The pain of separation deepened as the shadows of my unanswered inquiries stretched across the landscape of our shattered connection.

This wasn't the first time life had wielded its unpredictable hand in moments of vulnerability. The recurrent pattern of adversity, an unwelcome companion, resonated through the chapters of my existence. Yet, the unexpected turn of her departure cut through my defenses with a precision that surpassed any previous wound. She, the lodestar of my everything, the sanctuary sought in the chaos, had become the source of an inexplicable pain that defied the limits of my comprehension.

As the journey through the terrain of despair unfolded, an excruciating odyssey painted in hues of grief and loss, I grappled with the weight of unanswered questions and the haunting emptiness left in her wake. The unraveling of our shared narrative mirrored the relentless dance of life, unfurling in ways I could never have foreseen. In the melancholic crescendo of this chapter's conclusion, the shadows of sorrow and heartache cast a long, haunting pall over the canvas of our shared history, leaving me to navigate the ruins of what once held the promise of eternity.

CHAPTER FIFTEEN

ECHOES OF DESOLATION: THE HOLLOW TRIUMPH OF SUCCESS

I lingered in the limbo of anticipation, waiting for her return as the days stretched into an eternity. Each passing moment carried the weight of hope and longing, an ever-growing yearning that clung to the fragile threads of optimism. In the tapestry of time, I wove my expectations, dreaming of a day when the void left by her departure would be filled with the warmth of her presence. Yet, as the clock's relentless march continued, the elusive promise of her return remained an unfulfilled echo, a haunting melody that played in the recesses of my waiting heart.

In the realm between wakefulness and slumber, her presence permeated my nights as vivid dreams painted the canvas of my sleep. Each night unfolded like a bittersweet reverie, a mirage that teased the edges of reality. In the ethereal landscapes of dreams, I found solace, albeit fleeting, as she appeared in the ephemeral glow of the subconscious. Her laughter echoed through the corridors of my mind, a haunting melody that danced on the periphery of my waking thoughts. Yet, with every sunrise, the dream's ephemeral embrace melted away, leaving me to grapple with the stark reality of her continued absence.

In the desperate quest to banish her from the recesses of my thoughts, I embarked on a relentless journey to forget. I sought refuge in distractions, burying myself in the cacophony of daily life, hoping the clamor would drown out the echoes of her memory. Yet, like an indelible ink stain on the canvas of my mind, her presence lingered, refusing to be erased.

I delved into the realms of hobbies and passions, attempting to fill the void with pursuits that once brought joy. Yet, even the most immersive activities failed to eclipse the ache of her absence. The laughter of friends, the embrace of fleeting joys—all were mere placeholders in the empty spaces she once occupied.

As the calendar pages turned, I traversed different landscapes, hoping change would be the alchemy to erase her imprint. New faces, unfamiliar places, and the passage of time became my reluctant allies in this battle against the specter of her memory. But with each passing day, the specter seemed to grow, casting its long shadow over my attempts to find solace.

In the silent corridors of my solitude, I grappled with the paradox of forgetting someone who had become an indelible part of my being. The more I tried to escape the tendrils of her memory, the tighter they wound around the fragile architecture of my consciousness, weaving a tapestry of longing and heartache that refused to unravel.

In the intricate tapestry of my past, various relationships had woven their threads, each leaving its distinct mark on the canvas of my experiences. The echoes of Kajal's presence, a chapter explored in the annals of my history, had etched a unique narrative with its complexities and nuances. Yet, amidst the array of connections, none cast a shadow as enduring as Avani's.

Her imprint, like an indelible ink spill, seemed to seep into the very fibers of my being, defying the passage of time. The stories shared, the laughter echoed, and the shared moments with Avani became an inseparable part of my consciousness. Despite the varied relationships that preceded her, the task of erasing Avani from the tableau of my memories proved a Sisyphean endeavor.

The impossibility of her erasure spoke to the profound impact she had etched upon my soul—a sentiment unlike any I had encountered in the labyrinth of past connections. Avani, with her unique blend of presence and absence, became an indomitable force, rewriting the narrative in the poignant language of emotions that resonated through the corridors of my heart.

In the midst of Delhi's vibrant tapestry, my journey took an unexpected turn as I sought off-campus opportunities to forge a career path. The city's bustling streets and towering corporate buildings painted a picture of ambition and professional promise. It wasn't long before I secured a position in a multinational company—a position that, by conventional standards, represented success and financial prosperity.

The offer, with its high package and the prestige associated with a renowned corporation, should have been cause for jubilation. However, the corridors of achievement echoed with a muted celebration. The customary joy that accompanied such accomplishments seemed veiled by the haunting specter of personal turmoil that continued to cast its shadow.

As I stepped into the corporate landscape, adorned with success stories and ambitious dreams, the gravity of the achievement should have lifted my spirits. Instead, the professional triumphs acted as mere distractions, failing to drown out the persistent echoes of an intangible void within. The glittering allure of success was juxtaposed against the ever-present hollowness, a poignant reminder that some victories couldn't eclipse the losses etched in the fabric of the soul.

Delhi, with its dynamic energy and pulsating rhythm, reflected the paradox within. The city's vibrant life mirrored the stark incongruity of outward triumphs against the backdrop of inner disquiet. Despite the professional milestones, a palpable sense of yearning lingered—a silent acknowledgment that the pursuit of career heights couldn't fill the void left by intangible losses.

The dichotomy of walking the halls of professional accomplishment while grappling with personal turbulence created a narrative of contradiction. The city became both a backdrop and a metaphor, a space where career dreams collided with the complexities of the human heart. In the midst of towering structures and bustling markets, the journey to reconcile achievement with inner peace unfolded—a journey where the glittering facade of success struggled to conceal the poignant echoes of an unresolved past.

The very skill that once defined my adaptability, akin to a chameleon seamlessly blending into its surroundings, now seemed to wane. In the labyrinth of professional pursuits and personal struggles, the innate ability to acclimate to new environments began to lose its luster. The chameleon within, once adept at navigating the ever-shifting landscapes of life, found itself grappling with an internal discord that defied easy assimilation.

Each new setting, whether corporate corridors or the vibrant streets of Delhi, became a canvas where the chameleon within attempted to don its familiar hues. Yet, the harmonious transition, once a hallmark of my adaptability, now faced a subtle disruption. The effortless assimilation that characterized my interactions with diverse environments began to fray at the edges, revealing the strain of internal unrest.

The city's dynamism, instead of offering a canvas for the chameleon within to paint its adaptive strokes, became a reflective surface that mirrored the intricate conflicts within. The once-fluent dance between self and surroundings now encountered a dissonant note, as if the chameleon were searching for a stable ground amidst the whirlwind of change.

In the journey of career ascent and personal introspection, the chameleon's elusive ability to seamlessly become one with its surroundings seemed to falter. The very essence of adaptability, once second nature, now faced a nuanced struggle against the currents of evolving circumstances. The chameleon within, grappling with the complexities of the journey, yearned for a semblance of equilibrium in a world that seemed increasingly unpredictable.

In my quest to reclaim a semblance of control over my life, I sought the guidance of a psychiatrist. The hope was that professional intervention and the prescribed tablets would be the key to unlocking the labyrinth of internal struggles. However, the initial tablets proved ineffective in alleviating the weight of turmoil that persisted within.

Communicating my lack of progress, the psychiatrist opted to adjust the dosage, incrementally increasing it in an attempt to calibrate a remedy. Yet, as the dosage climbed, so did the side effects. The tablets, intended to serve as a lifeline, often left me suspended in a dilution state—a realm where the boundaries between reality and illusion became increasingly blurred.

Navigating daily life became a precarious dance on the tightrope of medication-induced haziness. The once-crystal-clear lines between clarity of thought and the fog of dilution now merged into an indistinct horizon. While the intention was to find solace in the realm of prescribed remedies, the unintended consequence was a descent into a twilight zone where the nuances of reality and perception intertwined in perplexing ways.

The journey toward mental well-being, initially guided by the hope of psychiatric intervention, became a delicate balance between seeking relief and grappling with the unsettling side effects that accompanied the pursuit of stability.

In the mundane rhythm of office life, I found myself submerged in a sea of faces, each interaction a reminder of the charm that once defined my social encounters. These people, though acquaintances, only knew the subdued version of me—the remnants of a person who had lost his vitality in the wake of Avani's departure. The real essence within, the vibrant core that used to animate my interactions, appeared to have evaporated, leaving behind a mere echo of the once lively individual.

As I traversed the corporate landscape, the dulled exterior became a canvas upon which the internal metamorphosis was etched. The radiant hues that once painted my persona in vivid shades had now faded, replaced by a muted and somber demeanor. The laughter that used to resonate in the corridors of my soul had been silenced, and the once vibrant energy had dissipated, leaving behind an emptiness that lingered.

Deep within, the sense of loss echoed through the caverns of my being—a poignant void where the memories of a love now lost reverberated. The psychiatrist's insight, suggesting that it might be easier for girls to forget than for a guy who had tasted the sweetness of true love, played like a haunting refrain in my emotional landscape. The weight of longing, the burden of unfulfilled promises, and the echo of a love once cherished created a complex tapestry of emotions that resisted fading away.

In the sea of people who now knew only the dulled version of me, the truth of my internal struggle remained concealed. The vibrant spirit that had once colored my existence had become a mere whisper, drowned out by the monotony of daily routines. Avani's departure had cast a shadow, one that seemed to stretch endlessly across the canvas of my life, eclipsing any possibility of a return to the vibrant hues that had once defined the chapters of love now confined to memory.

The psychiatrist's prescribed tablets, intended to be a beacon of stability, often felt like an anchor, tethering me to a dilution state where the boundaries between reality and illusion blurred. Navigating through the haze of medication-induced haziness became a precarious dance, where the once-clear lines between clarity of thought and the fog of dilution merged into an indistinct horizon.

In the city's dynamic embrace, where corporate ambitions collided with personal struggles, I found myself grappling with the dichotomy of walking the halls of professional accomplishment while facing the complexities of the human heart. The journey, initially set against the backdrop of glittering achievements, had encountered a nuanced struggle against the currents of evolving circumstances.

As I penned these reflections, the chapters of my life unfolded on the pages of memory. The love that had once painted my world in vibrant hues now existed as a cherished relic, its echoes resonating in the recesses of my heart. The vibrant spirit, once the guiding force of my journey, seemed to have taken refuge in the nostalgic corridors of the past.

And so, in this symphony of memories and melancholy, I decided to draw the curtain on this narrative. The chapters of love, loss, and the quest for self-discovery had played out against the canvas of life. As I closed this book, a sense of closure enveloped me—an acknowledgment that some stories find their conclusion in the quiet acceptance of what has been and the unwritten possibilities of what may come. The pen, once a vessel for the ink of emotions, now rested, and the story of love, with all its joys and heartaches, reached its final cadence.

Author's Note

Dear Readers,

"Chameleon Heart" is more than just a story—it's a piece of my soul, a reflection of the journey we all embark upon when we leave the nest and step into the world on our own. This novel encapsulates the myriad emotions, challenges, and triumphs that define our formative years.

Writing this book has been a deeply personal and cathartic experience. As I penned each chapter, I found myself reliving the excitement, heartbreak, and growth that come with the territory of young adulthood. My hope is that you, too, will find a piece of your own journey within these pages.

This story is dedicated to anyone who has ever felt the thrill of independence, faced the sting of failure, or discovered the strength within themselves to overcome life's obstacles. It's a testament to the resilience and adaptability we all possess, much like the chameleon that changes to survive and thrive.

I am deeply grateful to everyone who has supported me throughout this journey—my family, friends, and, most importantly, you, the readers. Your belief in this story has given it life and meaning. Thank you for allowing "Chameleon Heart" to become a part of your life.

May this book inspire you to embrace change, cherish every moment, and find strength in your journey.

With heartfelt thanks,

Anmol Ranjan

About The Author

Anmol Ranjan is a passionate writer and an accomplished professional in the field of computer science and information technology. After earning a B.Tech in Computer Science and Engineering from JECRC, Anmol began their career as an Analyst in Information Technology at HCL. Following a year of valuable experience, Anmol joined Infosys as a Senior Technical Process Executive, where they continued to deepen their expertise in providing support and gaining knowlege on computer network systems and cybersecurity.

Currently, Anmol is pursuing an MBA from IIT Patna, further expanding their knowledge and skills in the realm of business and technology. Despite a demanding professional and academic career, Anmol has always nurtured a profound passion for writing, a love that has been a constant companion since childhood.

With a strong presence on Instagram, Anmol connects with followers by sharing heartfelt reflections and insights. Writing has always been more than just a hobby; it is a way to pour out emotions and connect with others on a deeper level. "Chameleon Heart" stands as the most time-consuming and closest creation to Anmol's heart, embodying the imagination into pen and paper.

To everyone who has embarked on this journey through "Chameleon Heart," Anmol extends heartfelt gratitude and love. Thank you for being part of this story and for allowing these words to touch your lives.